Saints and Curses

Alexis Lantgen

www.lunarianpress.com

This book is a work of fiction. All the names, places, characters, and incidents are products of the author's lively imagination. Any resemblance to actual events, place, or people living or dead, is entirely coincidental.

For my beloved friends and family, especially my beautiful children.

You are my light in dark places.

Table of Contents

GRACKLE

Jane wasn't surprised when Michael pulled out his wand and brandished it at her. She had told him she wanted him to move out, and he could be volatile. After all, that's why she wanted him to move out in the first place.

She'd come prepared. She'd chosen a restaurant known for its magical barriers and purchased a counterspell from the drugstore. The spell came with a potion that smelled like off-brand hand cream and a charm that looked like a refrigerator magnet. It had an inspirational slogan scrawled across it that read "Just believe in yourself and your dreams will materialize," which was clearly written by someone who never remembered their dreams.

Nonetheless, the potion and the flimsy charm had given Jane enough confidence that she only stammered a little when she asked Michael to move out.

"I mean, neither of us is happy, right? It's not about you, we're just not good together, you know? Umm, I mean, you hate my friends, and the other day you called me boring."

He'd said other things as well, things she found too painful to repeat out loud, but boring seemed damning enough. She plucked at her skirt beneath the table, then darted a glance in Michael's direction to see how he was taking it.

He clenched his jaw, and he had gritted his teeth so hard she could hear them grinding. She stammered into a silence that stretched before her like an abyss.

Jane panicked. She wanted to take it all back, to tell him she didn't mean it, that she was wrong, stupid. But his gaze weighed down on her until her tongue felt too heavy to move. A small, rebellious, suicidally stupid part of her wondered if she wanted to take it all back anyway.

When he pulled out his wand, she was relieved. That's how it would be, then. But she had a spell he didn't know about and he couldn't do much in a restaurant anyway, could he? That's why she'd chosen a public place, like her mother had always said.

The spell he shot at her blasted away her meager charm. The heat of it burned her face. She ducked beneath the table, scrambling away as their waitress drew her wand to settle things down. But Michael was quick. He hurled another spell at her, one hot enough to set off the sprinkler system and summon the security gargoyles. It hit Jane in the back of her knee, the one that never seemed the same after she'd twisted it freshman year.

A flash of light. Blinding pain. Then the disorienting feeling of being entirely the wrong size, and weight, and shape. She threw her hands up, but she didn't have hands, only scraggly black wings.

Chaos surrounded her. One of the security gargoyles tackled Michael, snapping his wand in two. The police were called. The Magisterium was summoned. Jane flapped around the room. The people in the restaurant loomed over her like giants, hulking and terrifying. Some of them batted at her, shrieking. Others grabbed at her. One pulled out her tailfeather, which hurt. A breeze stirred around the room, and she saw an open window. She struggled towards it, flapping and hopping, but when she reached the windowsill, she hesitated and looked back.

"Even as a bird you're ugly!" Michael yelled. "Fucking ugly ass grackle--I should have--" A gargoyle clamped its heavy clay hand over his mouth, or maybe punched him in the face; it was hard to tell what it intended. Jane looked out the window, felt the breeze under her wings, and glided away.

It's not that she intended to stay a bird, forever cursed by her ex. But when she thought about going back to her and Michael's tiny, overpriced apartment or to the dreary grey building where she worked, she couldn't quite bring herself to do it. Especially when she thought about the enormous magical med bills she'd rack up to get back her human body. She'd have to file for bankruptcy or sell herself into thralldom. And the recent economic downturn had driven down the going rate for souls.

It wasn't so bad, at first. Like a vacation, but one of those gritty find-yourself-backpacking trips instead of the elegant Instagram kind. It took a lot of hops and falls to learn to fly, but once she figured out how to catch the thermals rising off the midday concrete, she could get airborne. Most of the time.

It was also the worst, like being homeless. In fact, it *was* being homeless. She didn't have a safe place to live as a bird. Who knew comfortable nests were so hard to build? Or that ninety percent of all "bird" houses were filled by irate squirrels?

Jane slept under the overhanging eaves of a different building every night, wherever she could find an available space. It was winter, and tree branches were stark and bare. Without a nest the cold wind cut its way through her fluffed feathers and she shivered.

And the hunger. She had been hungry before, usually when she tried a horrible new diet. But she had not known desperate hunger, hunger like a knife in the belly. She could eat a variety of foods in her new bird form, but it was all hard to get or so inedible she struggled to make herself swallow.

She tried choking down a beetle. It crunched like stiff plastic and oozed a bitter yellow pus. She hacked it up. Afterwards, Jane avoided insects, even if other birds ate them with relish. Instead, she picked at human leftovers, stealing food from trash cans or crumbs that had dropped on the ground. A few times she was lucky enough to meet a kind soul feeding birds in the park, and she gobbled offered bits of stale bread.

Even worse than hunger was the loneliness. Most humans didn't speak to her. The mad magicians who slept on the sidewalk recognized the spell binding her. They sometimes cackled to themselves as she flew by, but they had little to say beyond esoteric mumbling. None of them offered a counterspell, which was unsurprising considering their own magic had driven them mad. Their red-rimmed eyes and manic laughter unsettled her.

Jane couldn't talk to most of the real birds either, or else they didn't want to talk to her. Bird language was harder to learn than she'd thought, and they had a deeply complex social hierarchy she struggled to understand. They also had an enormous mistrust of humans, even those in bird form.

"We have tried to talk to ground walkers before," a chickadee told her, "but you understand nothing." He clicked his beak in slow, exaggerated motions so she could keep up with his words. Jane wondered if he was mocking her.

"I understand you now," she said. She hated the awkward caws and clicks she made when she tried to speak the bird language. She imagined it must be the bird equivalent of stuttering or slurring her words, or at the least very bad grammar. The chickadee cringed a bit listening to her.

"Nothing," he repeated, hopping for emphasis. "Nothing."

So, Jane didn't speak to anyone at all, not much anyway, and the loneliness hurt like a shard of ice lodged in her heart. Had she still been human, she would have been too depressed to get out of bed in the morning, or at all. She probably would have hidden under a thick warm quilt for the rest of her life, or until someone evicted her from her apartment.

But Jane wasn't human anymore, and the eaves and rooftops where she slept were too cold and too noisy to tempt her to hide there long.

"I need to get out of the city," she thought. "Migrate somewhere nicer."

Migration, however, is long and treacherous, and Jane didn't really have the fat reserves or the flying ability she needed to make the journey. Instead, she made her way to a city park.

The park she found was on the edges of a small lake (more of a largish pond, really) fed by a minimally polluted stream. To a human, the park would likely seem small, neglected, and disappointing. The trees were scraggly. The pond had murky water and sludgy shores that smelled like duck poop and rotten eggs. Clumps of yellow-brown grass grew tall and itchy in the muck. The only wildlife seemed to be woebegone ducks and a handful of scrawny black and brown grackles.

To Jane, the park was wondrous. Trees towered above her bird form as awesome as the mightiest redwoods. The thick grasses muffled noise from the street, creating a quiet unknown to most of the city. If humans found the park disappointing, all the better for the grackles--it became their space, a haven. Jane loved it.

She had never managed to build a nest with the stringy, much-trampled sidewalk grass, but the thick, strong reeds that grew in the rich mud were perfect. She watched other grackles and even the ducks to learn their nest-building secrets. After three failed prototypes, Jane's fourth attempt held together. Her nest was small, and not quite as neat as the other birds'. But it was snug and warm, and it felt safe. And it was her own, made by her own talons with grass and reeds she'd collected herself. As she curled up in her nest for the first time, Jane felt a sense of peace for the first time in years.

It was several days after she'd built her nest that Jane met Ki. At first glance, Ki looked like a typical raven--glossy black feathers, strong wings, and a thick, powerful beak. On a closer look, Ki's black eyes gleamed with intelligence, both mischievous and wise. His iridescent wings gave off faint blue crackles of magic when he laughed. And he had a subtle accent to his speech--a human accent.

Jane did not dare approach him. Large birds like ravens preyed on grackles like her, though it was rare among park birds and considered uncivilized. Anyway, what would he want with a bird like her? Jane had been ordinary all her life, ugly and boring, like Michael had said. His words blazed in her mind, even when she tried to forget. She buried her head under her wing.

The first time Ki spoke to her, Jane was digging through human trash, looking for crumbs. She hadn't noticed his approach, or she would have flown away. Instead, she gradually became aware of his presence. She looked up, a limp French fry hanging from her beak. Ki had an apple core in his bill, only a little browned. Jane looked at it with longing--fresh fruit was hard to find in the dull brown winter months, and she had not

6

had any in a long time. Ki gripped the core between his bill and one powerful talon, then ripped it in two with a twist of his beak. One of the pieces he tossed to her, and the other he bit. It made a juicy crunch.

Jane hopped toward the offered fruit. It looked delicious, and Ki did not seem to be hovering over it. She took a tentative bite, then pecked at it with indulgent joy.

"I found it under the picnic tables by the old birch," Ki said.

Jane didn't answer right away, partly because her beak was full and partly because she was stunned he was talking to her.

"Thank you," she croaked. She took another beakful of apple to hide her embarrassment.

"No worries," he said. He peered at her, turning his head quizzically. "What is your name?"

She hopped and dipped her head. "Jane."

"Jane," he repeated. His deep caw made her name sound exotic and powerful, a witch's name, not the plain one she'd been labelled with all her life. "You are magical."

She bobbed her head again, uncertain. "No," she said. "I am cursed."

"I see a spell," Ki said, looking at her with shining black eyes. "But a weak one. It would not be strong enough to hold you if you did not feed it your power."

Jane fluffed her wings. "I did not choose this form," she said.

"Why not?" Ki asked. "It is glorious. You are capable of flight but can hide easily. You can survive. You can find peace. Is that not so?"

"I am not beautiful."

"A peacock is beautiful, but his tail weighs him down so he cannot fly, and it calls predators to him."

"I would like to be human again," she said.

7

"Would you?" Ki asked, and suddenly Jane wasn't sure. She hopped and flapped her wings, pecking at the last of the apple. When it was gone, she flew away. Ki did not try to follow her.

That night, snug in her nest, Jane had a dream. She and Michael were arguing about the new lamps she'd bought for their apartment. They had short, rounded bases and ordinary fixtures, the out-of-date kind of lamps sold at garage sales or thrift shops. Michael mocked them for being "pedestrian." She felt her shoulders slump, and the hot blush spread across her face. She was stupid. He was right they looked...but she saw them again and remembered why she'd bought them in the first place. The lampshades had a pattern of small brown birds, bright happy things sitting in nests, flying, or singing. They'd looked joyful, even in a cardboard box on a shelf in a garage. She reached out and touched one, and it felt soft and alive. The little lamp bird opened its beak, as though to tell her something important that she'd forgotten.

She woke up. Her nest was coated in a sprinkle of early morning dew, delicate drops clinging to the reeds of her home. Tears, Jane thought, but she couldn't tell if they were happy or sad.

"If I'm magical," she said to Ki that afternoon, "then why can't I change back?" They'd met by the picnic tables, which were indeed full of fruits and rich crumbs from some of Jane's favorite foods.

"Magic is the heart's manifest," Ki said. "It is the song of the soul and the fruit of desire. Ergo, you cannot shed your cloak of feathers unless you truly desire a human form or a human life."

"Why you don't go back?"

8

He looked at her, and his eyes were black and shining and sad. Then he lifted his head and fluffed the feathers on his neck and wings. He looked strong and proud, wild and wise.

"There is no place for me in the human world," he said.

Jane wondered if she'd offended him and he'd fly away, but he didn't. He spent a few moments cleaning his feathers while she pecked at the leftover pieces of coffee cake stuck to a paper plate.

"If you want to go back," Ki said after a bit of silence. "You need to find something or someone to draw you back. A desire for human connection, maybe. I went back to visit my grandmother sometimes before she passed."

"Could you show me?"

Ki reached his wings toward the sky, his flight feathers outstretched like long, elegant fingers. He grew, his body extending into a glistening bridge between the earth and sky. His feathers melted together, and his beak softened and widened into lips.

Ki was a man and still beautiful, Jane thought. His arms were lithe and strong, his skin dark and smooth. He stood with the grace of a dancer. His eyes were the same, wild and black. He smiled, yet something about his expression broke her heart.

"Do you see, little one?" Ki knelt and held out his hand. Jane hopped onto one of his fingers, turning her head from side to side.

"You are magnificent," she chirped. "Who were you before?"

"Ahh," Ki said. "That is a story for another day." He set her down and gave a graceful leap, his arms outstretched like wings. And then they were wings, and Ki was a raven once more.

9

Jane looked at him closely. She had not noticed the fineness of his talons before, how agile they were.

"Were you a dancer?"

"Sometimes." Ki spread his wings so that they glistened in the sunlight and lifted his beak to the sky. "But other times I washed dishes in the back of a Chinese restaurant. Dancing doesn't pay the bills, unless...well, let's just say there's dignity in washing dishes. What did you do, before?"

Jane ducked her head under her wing. "Whatever I could to survive, really." She'd had so much debt, and she had gotten stuck as an unpaid intern at several jobs before giving up and taking whatever job could pay her through the temp agency.

"But what did you want to do?"

"Nothing realistic," she said. She pecked at some stale crumbs. "Writing, art, making things. I liked to sing, too, but I wasn't good at it. It's stupid, really. None of the things I loved could ever make me any money."

"Love isn't about money."

"Survival is."

"Only when you're human."

"Is that why you don't go back?"

"It's one reason, and a good one."

"Yeah." Jane scratched in the dirt. Her bird feet made tiny footprints in the dust, like funny little fork marks. "It's lonely though. Could I have a family as a bird? Wouldn't it be weird to--you know--with another bird? And what about my children? Or chicks, I guess. Would they be humans in bird form or just birds or I don't know, some weird combination?"

Ki made a gurgling croak, which Jane thought might be laughing. "I don't know," he said.

"I want to turn back someday," she said.

"But not right now?"

She spread her wings. She found the cushion of warm air rising off the concrete and caught it with her long flight feathers. No, not right now, she thought, and she rose high above the park, above the city. A couple of rooftop falcons eyed her with lazy interest, but they had caught a fat pigeon and did not seem interested in another hunt. She could enjoy the air and revel in the feel of its complex currents beneath her wings.

Spring brought at least a few humans to the park. Homeless men and women, some of them magicians, slept on the benches at night. But they retreated during the day, leaving the park to the nannies and young mothers.

It was a time of great feasting for the birds, because toddlers love scattering crumbs about them wherever they go. Jane and the other grackles followed them from a safe distance, waiting for clumsy fingers to shower the ground with unwanted bits of cookie or bread or crispy snacks. On some lucky days an irate child might even throw a tantrum and reward the grackles' patience with entire cups or bowls or even trays of food.

"You're wasting it!" the nannies and mothers would scold, but anyone who watches birds knows that dropped food is rarely wasted.

Jane liked watching the children. Once, in her life before, she'd wanted to become a kindergarten teacher.

"But you're so talented," her mother had moaned. "Why would you waste your life on such a dead-end job?"

"Why?" Michael had said. "So, you can make even less money than you do now?"

"I could learn to take care of children," she'd said. "It might be useful if we ever--"

11

"I don't want kids," he'd snapped. "Ever."

Jane's favorite child at the park was a round-faced two or three-year-old with fuzzy black braids called Maribel. She came to the park with an indifferent teenage girl Maribel called "Tia," who may have been her nanny, her sister, or even her mother for all Jane could tell. Tia spent most of her time at the park staring at her cell phone, doling out a steady supply of graham crackers and goldfish to Maribel whenever the little girl tried to get her attention.

As a grackle, Jane had become a connoisseur of crackers, and Maribel was very generous as toddlers went. But the child was appealing in other ways too. She never tried to grab feathers or run at a flock to see them scatter. She sang to Jane in a sweet, nonsense way. For those reasons, and because Maribel was often lonely, Jane played with her. She'd hop close to the little girl's feet and sometimes even take food out of her hand. She'd "talk" to her in bird language. Maribel would nod along, though Jane was sure the little girl couldn't really understand what she said. Fairly sure.

As spring bled into summer, the city suffered a brutal heat wave. The concrete glittered like desert sand, and even the ancient, dried up pieces of gum along the sidewalks grew melty and sticky again. Maribel played in the dry, browned grass near the pond, Sweat beaded on her forehead. She begged Tia for a popsicle from the street cart, but Tia waved her off with a couple of graham crackers. She ate one of these in silence and crumpled the other into a little pile of crumbs for Jane.

"Firsty?" Maribel said. Tia pointed at a creaky, rusted water fountain near the park bench. Maribel clambered over and pushed the button. The fountain made a scratchy chugging noise, released a tiny spray of water, then went dry.

"Firsty?" Maribel asked again. Tia shrugged and stared at her phone.

Jane pecked halfheartedly at the graham crumbs then flew away. It was too hot to eat, even graham crackers. She was drowsing on a branch near the pond when something pricked her attention. She lifted her head, turning it this way and that, a cold feeling settling in her gizzard despite the heat of the day. Maribel sat on the edge of the pond. The little girl had taken off her pink shoes with the yellow flowers, and one soft little foot inched towards the water.

The pond wasn't usually deep, but it was swollen with spring rains, and the banks were soft and waterlogged. The bank crumbled beneath the little girl's weight and toppled her into the water. Maribel panicked. She struggled to stand up and reach the edge but slipped on the sticky muck and got tangled in the water weeds. She kicked and struggled to free herself. She made one desperate wail, then fell silent, her arms pumping to try to lift her head above water.

Jane had never felt so helpless. She flew over Maribel's head, but she was too small to pull her out. She glanced over at Tia, still on her phone. Even if she got Tia's attention, she had no way to tell her what was happening. She squawked and shrieked, but no one was close enough to hear her.

Defeated, Jane landed near the shore. Maribel struggled. Her head slipped under the water, and her movements grew feeble.

Jane reached out her wing like an arm, and it grew longer. She felt her feathers lengthen into fingers, her legs sprout, and her feet bloom. She had been hopping anxiously. Now she knelt on the shore, the weight and strength and size of her body strange and familiar.

She stepped unsteadily into the water. Maribel had slipped beneath the surface, and she'd churned up so much silt it was hard to see. Jane waded out to where she had last seen the girl. There was a flutter of movement near her leg. She took a deep breath and plunged beneath the surface, feeling around the muddy bottom. She felt a brush of hair. She grasped it, found the girl's shoulders and head, and pulled her up.

They broke the surface. Jane hauled Maribel out of the water. She was limp and heavy, and Jane couldn't hear breathing or see her chest move. She lay the little girl on her back and tried to remember what she'd learned about CPR in health class. Chest compressions, thirty of them, then two breaths. Repeat.

Nothing happened. She was too late. Chest compressions--

A weak cough. Sputtering breath. Tears rolled down Jane's face. Real tears--she hadn't felt them in a long while. Birds can't cry.

Tia cried too. "What's wrong, what's wrong, I'm so sorry, I'm going to be in so much trouble, oh my god, Maribel!"

Tia called 911. Jane stepped back. She wondered if she should stay for the ambulance, but when she looked down, she realized she was completely nude. A consequence of living as a wild animal, she supposed. Tia turned to her, mouth agape.

"I'll just be going," Jane said. She yearned for the sky and escape, and black feathers sprouted from her skin. She stretched towards the sky and flew. She circled the skies, waiting for the ambulance to arrive.

"You're lucky someone got to her so fast," the EMT said after she and her partner had seen to Maribel. "She looks like she'll make a full recovery. Did you have to do CPR?"

14

"I didn't, but there was someone else--she, uh, left," Tia said. She stared at the birds on a nearby bench, shaking her head.

Jane soared overhead. It was time, she thought. She was ready.

A few years later, Tia waited to pick up Maribel from her first day of school. The little girl came running up to her.

"I love my teacher!" Maribel said. She had grown several inches and her face had lost some of its baby roundness, but she had the same fuzzy braids. "Look what she gave me!"

"A paper crane!" Tia said, putting down her phone. "It's beautiful." She glanced at the new kindergarten teacher, an ordinary young woman with a plain face and mousy hair. Then she looked again.

"Have we met before?" Tia asked.

"I don't think so," Jane said. "But it's nice to meet you. Maribel is a pleasure to have in class."

Maribel smiled at her teacher. "Ms. Jane is so beautiful! And she can fly!" She took Jane's hand. "Will you show me? Can I learn to fly too?"

"Maybe someday," Jane said. She smiled, wild and joyful, and her hair floated in the breeze like feathers.

Lantgen

ELVEN CAROLS

The worst part of my job had to be the costume. The tunic and tights were a nauseating shade of neon green. The shoes looked like something a deranged jester would wear. The natty red "elf" hat was trimmed in mangy rabbit fur that upset my allergies. I'd sneezed so much my nose had turned bright red; I looked more like Rudolph the Red-Nosed Reindeer than any self-respecting elf. It didn't help that I was standing in the middle of a particularly tacky Christmas display in a shopping mall, playing carols on my violin while obnoxious kids stuck candy canes in my hair. All in all, quite a horrible holiday job. Still, since I was pretty much a starving artist, emphasis on the starving, I needed the cash.

I didn't notice the funny little people until I took my break after a three-hour set. They were standing close to my spot, poking at the decorations with looks of disapproval and bafflement. There were five of them, three men and two women, and none were over five feet tall. They had ruddy cheeks and odd clothes--breeches and full skirts decorated with fine embroidery, the type of stuff I'd imagine high class

Medieval peasants might wear. The women had elaborately braided hair, and the men all wore long beards. I was impressed--they must've come from a way nicer display than mine.

I finished my break and started warming up for my next set. I'd played the same songs so often I had to invent challenges to keep myself from going mad from boredom. This time, I thought, I'll play everything transposed up a fifth. But before I could begin my performance, one of the little men hopped over the balding velvet rope intended to keep mobs of shoppers well back from the scenery.

"Ummm, I don't think you should be back here," I told him.

"Oh Fa La La La La, don't mind that now. I need to talk to you," he said, stroking his long black beard.

"You do? I mean... I have to get back to work now." I struggled to remember the rest of the script my boss insisted I repeat every time a customer got "overcome with the Holiday Spirit" and pushed their way onto the set. It happened at least once a shift, but usually the culprits were sugar-crazed tots or elderly grandmas blinded by the blinking lights.

"Remember that Santa and all his elves are very busy this time of year, so it's best to let us do our jobs...and don't forget the fabulous Christmas specials going on today at, ummm, Tim's Sporting Goods, where Christmas is a ball." I blushed at how stupid I sounded, but what are you going to do? It's a job.

The little man leveled me with a look of complete disdain. "Santa and his elves? Are you kidding me? Holly and Ivy, this is a travesty. But never mind. Listen, I need to talk to you about something important. Meet us at..." he looked around as if trying to find the least offensive place in a sea of fluorescent lights and tinsel. "Tea Garden Express."

"You want to meet me in the Chinese restaurant?"

"Yes, yes. Immediately after your...shift...if you please. Ask for Grumplebumble."

I thought for a second. These guys might be crazed fans of shopping mall music, but they seemed harmless enough. "Only if you're buying, eh, Grumblebumple..."

"Grumplebumble. Of course, of course. See you then." He skipped (and I mean literally skipped) back to his comrades and they vanished into the crowd.

Maybe I was inspired by my visit with the strange little man, but my next set sounded amazing. I swear, my version of "Jingle Bell Rock" had kids dancing in manic little circles, and my "O Come, O Come Emmanuel" had tired moms dabbing at their eyes. It almost made up for the vomit that sprayed all over my shoes when one of the kids got dizzy from the dancing. The subdued brown spots even complimented their lurid green and red stripes. At least, they couldn't possibly make them worse. Still, by the end of my performance I couldn't wait to escape to Tea Garden Express, which was blessedly free of tinsel, garlands, and sleigh bells.

The funny little man and his cohorts sat at a booth near the back of the restaurant, poring over the menu as though it were written in, well, Chinese.

I heard one of their party, a tiny golden-haired woman, say "The servant girl tells me they have roast duck here, which is like to the roast fowls we eat on feast days." The rest of the group nodded, and a grumpy looking waitress rushed off to the kitchen.

"Ahhh, there she is! A muse of the viol!" Grumplebumble said, waving at me to come sit down. The other little people jostled around me, shaking my hands and scooting over to give me room. In truth, they were so small, that although the booth was only meant for four, there was plenty of room for all six of them and me. The table came up to their necks, making them look like a row of jolly holiday bobble heads.

"Welcome," Grumplebumble said. "We brought you here because we need a musician for our great yuletide feast, and the old Magnusbach badly wanted a viol player. We'd nearly given up hope of finding one, when we heard your dulcet tones playing in this...indoor marketplace. You certainly played our ancient melodies with great verve!"

"Thank you," I replied. However strange these little people were, it's always nice when someone appreciates my music. And if they were offering me a job, all the better. "So, I'll need some more details on the gig. What day, what time, how long you need me to play, that sort of thing. And of course, how much do you pay?"

Grumplebumble rubbed his chin and exchanged a look with the little red-bearded man on his left. The red beard passed a piece of parchment--actual parchment--across the table to me.

"We have listed all the details here. Will...er...three hundred suffice?"

"That should do nicely," I replied. I tried to play it cool, but at that moment I would have played almost any amount of violin for three hundred dollars. Still, I looked over the contract carefully--it never hurt to be cautious. "Tir Na Nog? I've never heard of the place. How do I get there?"

"Fear not, we shall send someone to escort you there when the time draws near. We do have one last request, though. The clothes at this party...well, we'd prefer you not wear the ensemble that you have on now."

"Don't worry about that." I'd be grateful if I could never wear this costume ever again, I thought.

"Good! Grismeldina here is our seamstress," he nodded at the tiny golden-haired woman. "And if you accept our contract, she can take your measurements and make you far more appropriate attire."

"Oh, uh, thanks." I was not looking forward to having to wear another costume. I could only pray it'd be less tacky than my current neon-green monstrosity.

"Excellent! Now remember, our feast is on the winter solstice; it begins at sundown and continues until we greet the dawn. You are to play the ancient carols while we feast and exchange gifts, then accompany the evening chorale. After that, you are free to enjoy the festivities before you return to your homeland."

"If you want to return," Grismeldina added.

"If she can return," said one of the little men as he stroked his long white beard.

"Oh, no, no, no, that won't be a problem, I assure you. So long as she follows the procedures. But perhaps she'll want to stay, or at least come back. We can always use fiddlers," Grumplebumble said.

All this talk about staying permanently at their little get together had me a tad alarmed. "I'm sure that Tir Na Nog is a lovely place, but I can't really stay there indefinitely. I've got a fiance, and a cat, and ummm, an apartment and all." This gig was seriously strange, but whatevs. Weird little people convinced that they were real elves are still way better than my typical clients--entitled bridezillas and creepy mall managers. Or so I hoped.

"Just don't eat any of the food," the white bearded man assured me, smiling kindly.

"And sign the contract," Grumplebumble said. He handed me a feathered quill and a pot of ink. I looked at it curiously for a second before scrawling my signature at the bottom of the parchment.

"Hurrah!" Grismeldina cheered. "We will start sewing your festival attire immediately. Willowflower, take her measurements. Peasebottom, fetch me some velvet ribbons to match the shade of her eyes!"

"Right away, Good Lady!" two of the little people answered. Before I knew what was happening, I was surrounded by measuring tapes, ribbons, and good-natured tailors.

"The things I do for my art," I moaned inwardly.

The day of the gig, I took off work early so I could get cleaned up by the time my ride arrived. I was nervous--after all, I'd never been to the restaurant the little people had talked about, or even heard of it. The name "Tir Na Nog" sounded so silly I figured the place had to be an ultra trendy hipster spot that only served lemons, tofu, and artfully arranged artisan cocktails made from whole-wheat gluten-free beer.

I leapt off the couch at the sound of a knock on my door. It was Peasebottom, a rosy-cheeked little man with nut-brown hair and a beard that fell past his knees. He waved merrily.

"Good afternoon, muse of the viol, and many blessings to you this fine feast day. I have not brought any rainbows, so we will be traveling by alicorn."

I let my eyebrows twitch, but otherwise kept a straight face. Rather than ask too many stupid questions, I just gave him a smile and nod. "I've got my violin and a good amount of sheet music, so I'm ready to roll."

"No, no, we won't be rolling at all, only riding. On Gingersnap! On Cloud-Dancer!" he called, loud enough to startle my cat. He danced a silly little jig, then hopped out the nearest window.

I gasped and rushed to see if Peasebottom had fallen to his death. But outside my window were two unicorns with large wings on their backs. I blinked and shook my head. I took a few puffs off my inhaler. But when I looked outside, they were still there. The sun gleamed off their silver feathers as the two unicorns hovered in complete defiance of the laws of physics. I heard a small child laughing and clapping from the sidewalk below, but though she pointed eagerly at the unicorns, none of the adults paid them the least bit of attention.

"Come now, don't be shy! Gingersnap here is a lovely creature, and she'll take good care to keep you from falling. Just hop on and grab hold of her mane," Peasebottom said in what I'm sure was meant to be a reassuring tone. "I'll carry your violin and things since you're not used to flying." He took my instrument out of my sweaty hands. I probably would've protested more, but shock does funny things to you.

I gulped. "Are you sure this is safe?"

"Of course it is. Nothing bad has ever happened to anyone while riding a unicorn... except for that one time..."

"What!" I gripped the window ledge.

"Mmmm, it seems we have a reluctant flyer. Well, no matter. Gingersnap, if you please." Peasebottom waved his hand. One of the unicorns darted its head towards the window, caught a bit of my shirt on its horn, then tossed me onto its back with a flick of its noble head. I never would have imagined a ravishingly beautiful unicorn could look so unbearably smug.

"Away we go!" Peasebottom called cheerily. The unicorns swooped around, flying at a speed that was equal parts terrifying and nauseating. I clung to that glittery horse and buried my face in its mane. It smelled like sweet jasmine, which under the circumstances only made me more nauseous.

Luckily, the journey didn't take long. I didn't dare look around or even take my face out of Gingersnap's mane until I was sure she had all four feet on the ground. When I finally looked around, I found I couldn't speak.

Have you ever seen those modelled little Christmas villages people put out around the holidays? The ones with tiny people ice-skating on glass ponds or shopping in adorably quaint shops? It was as if I had shrunk down in the middle of one of those. Hordes of jolly little people (not people, I realized--*elves*) dressed in brilliantly colored Christmas sweaters and singing joyfully pressed around me. I stood nearly two feet taller than everyone in my vicinity. Despite these crowds, the snow was so white, it *sparkled*--and I meant really sparkled as if it came right out of a toothpaste commercial.

I sat there dumbly for a few minutes until Gingersnap nudged at me with her nose. When I still didn't move, Peasebottom's unicorn poked me with her horn.

"Ouch! Alright, I'm going!" I said. I slid off my unicorn into the soft, powdery snow.

"Welcome, welcome! May the snow always cushion your falls!" It was Grumplebumble. He helped me out of the snow. "The preparations for the feast are already well under way. Let me escort you to Grismeldina--she has made lovely and highly fashionable clothes for you." With that, he led me along the main street towards a large, round hill. Peasebottom trailed behind us with my music and instrument. The violin looked so large in his arms I might as well have played cello.

As we reached the hill, I saw it had an opening to a cave or tunnel. We entered the passage, and it was as though we entered a medieval palace. Except it wasn't a palace exactly. It was huge, no doubt, but unlike palaces, which seem cold or distant or uncomfortably fancy, this place was homey and gay. It had red ribbons and bright green wreaths with real, live birds singing in them. There were Christmas trees that seemed to grow right out of the ground. they were ornamented with everything you could imagine--shining silver and gold stars, brightly colored sparrows and squirrels that sang and hopped, delicate balls of spun sugar, and golden-eyed foxes that peered out from the branches. Instead of carpet, the floor was covered in the finest, softest green moss I'd ever seen.

Grumplebumble took me to an enormous banquet hall full of elves bustling about. They were heaping a table with heavy trays of delicious-looking food. I tried to grab a cookie, but Grumplebumble hurriedly slapped my hand away.

"No, no, you can't eat yet--the guests will be arriving any minute and we must have music. And anyway...well, that's a matter for another time. Here, this is the Great Magnusbach. He will tell you what to do." He introduced me to an ancient elf with a white beard long enough for him to trip over.

"May the stars shine on our meeting, human child," the Magnusbach intoned. He bowed politely. Unsure what to do, I nearly fell over attempting an awkward curtsy. I flushed, but the Magnusbach's eyes twinkled. He took my hand, which helped me to steady myself.

"We have a music stand for you here," the Magnusbach pointed at a beautifully carved wooden stand. It was too low to the ground for me to use comfortably. Noticing this, the elderly elf pulled out a curved stick, rather like a conductor's baton, and tapped it three times. The wood grew until the stand sat at just the right height.

"Thank you," I said. I tried to shake myself awake--everything was so magical I felt as though I'd slipped into a dream.

"There you are! And not a moment to spare! When were you going to bring her to me, you fluffy-headed cotton-beard?" A commanding voice interrupted my reverie. Grismeldina, the elven clothier who'd taken my measurements before, strode towards us. She radiated a grim and intense practicality.

"Imagine, her performing for the Yuletide feast dressed in such a bizarre human fashion! And after all the work we put in, making elegant attire in such an enormous size..."

"I'm not enormous! I'm...human-sized," I protested. Truthfully, I looked like a giant standing next to the tiny, elderly Magnusbach and this diminutive seamstress.

"Hmmph." Grismeldina sniffed. "You! Go fetch me her shoes! Look sharp!" She pointed her finger at Grumplebumble, who looked a bit put out at being ordered around. Nonetheless, he snapped to attention and hustled out the door. "And you! We need bells! More bells!" With a flick of her wrist, she sent Peasebottom scurrying off.

"Bring her back before the candlefall," Magnusbach told her. He bowed politely and seemed more amused than insulted by Grismeldina's interruption.

"Now quickly, you must come to the dressing rooms. We have many fine ladies to attire this evening, and you may pose

26

some difficulties due to your, er, humansizedness." She took my elbow with a surprising amount of strength for a tiny elf, and half pulled me towards a small door behind one of the larger Christmas trees.

I sighed and trudged along rather grudgingly. I'd really hoped they'd forgotten about the damn costume they were going to make me wear.

In the end, it wasn't as bad as I feared. It was far worse. Grismeldina's sewing was impeccable and the dress she made, a rich green velvet in the elven style with gorgeous golden embroidery, was lovely beyond anything I'd ever seen in the real, er, human world (I later learned elves do not like us referring to our world as "real." After all, their world is every bit as real to them as ours is to us. This is one of the things humans do that elves find offensive). But the dressing rooms were small even by elf standards, and so I was crammed into a space the size of a large cardboard box with several frazzled elven maids who proceed to tug, pull, button and stuff me into elegant finery. One intrepid lass climbed up my back where she took hold of my unruly hair and tamed it into an elaborate braid with ribbons and tiny silver bells. I jingled every time I turned my head too far. At last, two burly elven matrons hoisted each of my feet into the air and shoved them into a pair of soft leather shoes. The toes curled up into narrow points that were tipped with more bells. Grismeldina strode over, gave me a quick inspection, and nodded fiercely.

"She's ready. Merry yuletide, human." Grismeldina snapped her fingers, and the burly elven matrons pushed me out the door, which snapped shut behind me. Unfortunately, the matrons had forgotten about the enormous Christmas tree that stood so close, and their last shove had sent me flying right into its branches. I got tangled in a lovely garland of holly and ivy, and accidentally stepped on a fox's tail. It bit my ankle.

"Ouch!" I yelped. Luckily, this brought old Magnusbach to help me. He was kind enough not to laugh, though his eyes twinkled far too much for my wounded pride.

"Well, at least now no one will object to your outlandish attire," he said. "And you're ready just in time! The grand procession will begin in a few minutes."

The Magnusbach took me to a small, slightly elevated stage I hadn't noticed before. My music was arrayed across the carved wooden stand. I wasn't alone on stage--there was a choir of tiny elven children warming up near me, and an elderly elf accompanying them on an ancient harpsichord. Magnusbach pressed a piece of parchment into my hands.

"I wrote out the melodies for the lollipop choir's songs. They will sing at the start of dinner. You can accompany them if you wish," then he pulled me down low to whisper, "please try to drown them out as much as possible!"

I nodded. The teeny children were rehearsing a song that sounded like "Silent Night" as arranged by Charles Ives.

"You begin playing after the horn call, and the choir director will signal you for the children's songs. You may accompany the communal singing that takes place after the feast, if you'd like. And most importantly, *don't eat any of the food*! I have taken the liberty of procuring some human food for you if you need a snack." He gestured proudly at an elegantly carved wooden bowl surrounded by a gorgeous wreath of holly. It was filled to the brim with artfully arranged twinkies.

"Twinkies? Really?" I gazed longingly at platters heaped with piping hot pies, glistening glazed roasts, and crisp brown turkeys. "Are you sure I can't have just one..."

"No," he interrupted. "It's not your time yet. You'd probably regret it immediately. Just don't eat the food."

"Okay," I sighed. I figured it's best not to argue with the clients.

At that moment, a hush filled the cavernous hall. A trio of elves marched towards the largest Christmas tree carrying golden horns. They climbed onto a small dais in front of the lush evergreen, lifted their horns, and played the most soul-soaring horn call I'd ever heard, and I've been in the orchestra for *Siegfried's Journey to the Rhine*. The crowd gave a huge cheer when they were done, and that was my cue to start performing.

I can't remember all the songs I played that night. The old Magnusbach had slipped me some heart-rending carols I'd never heard before. I felt like I existed in a realm of pure music, and my violin joined a great orchestra of the earth and stars. Even the children's choir managed a beautiful performance--their mistakes gave the music a touching poignance it might not have otherwise had. And the dancing! The elves danced so lightly and joyfully, I felt as though I could have watched them forever. Had I joined in the dance, I might not have wanted to leave.

I remember Grumplebumble had tears in his eyes as I played a particularly haunting melody. When I finished the song, he clapped wildly, then snatched a choice-looking blueberry tart from the table and handed it to me.

"For your song," he said. "A musician's soul belongs here."

I hurriedly took the tart before the Magnusbach could see, but he caught me and took it away. Then he gave Grumplebumble a stern look. "It should be her choice, not a trick," he said. Grumplebumble looked a bit sheepish.

After that, the night start to slip by like a dream. I remember exquisite music, a beautiful swirl of colors, and a feeling of deep joy. I must have fallen asleep at one point, or fallen into some kind of trance, because I remember waking up at the first light of dawn. The great hall had grown quiet; many of the elves were slumped over the feast table, fast asleep, and others rubbed their eyes blearily. There were a few dancers left, but their movements had become slow and languid. Rosy fingers of light glowed from the grand entrance.

The old Magnusbach sat quietly at my elbow. Unlike everyone else, he seemed wide awake. In the pale light he looked as warm and venerable as a Renaissance portrait.

"Did you enjoy the yuletide feast?" he asked. His smile was kind, but his eyes looked serious.

"It was..." I searched for words. I was still half-asleep from the night before. "It was awesome!" Okay, maybe not my best moment, but I'm a musician, not a poet.

He laughed. "Indeed, it was. I felt as though you belonged here, and many others felt the same way. But feelings can be misleading." He paused and stroked his long white beard.

"What I am about to tell you is a great secret. There are many humans who've tried to find us or force their way here to take our riches or our magic. Some have succeeded. So long ago we made a great magic that protects the lands we have left. That is why no one from your human world sees us, unless we want them too."

I nodded, still bleary eyed. It made sense.

"Sometimes, though, we want humans to visit us, and here the magic takes a strange turn. I think one of the ancestors was afraid that if our human visitors left, they would lead others back here. Or perhaps the magic only calls its own home and roots them to this place. Whatever the reason, if a human eats any of our food, they can--in fact they must--return here and stay forever."

I sucked in my breath. "I kind of gathered something was up with the food. So, if I'd eaten any of it..."

"You could never leave," the Magnusbach said. "I would have told you last night, but I feared that under the influence of our joyous revelry, you'd make a rash decision."

I felt dizzy for a moment. It had been an incredible night, but I had a fiancee, cats, and parents who would miss me if I just disappeared. Yet, part of me almost wished I had eaten the food. I'd ridden a unicorn and played music with elves. I'd fallen a little in love with this place.

"You would be welcome to stay here, of course, but I think it's not the right time yet. So I'm giving you a gift instead. You must keep it secret and never tell a living soul who does not share your blood." He searched in his pocket for a moment, and pulled out a small, brown acorn. "This is a nut from our oldest tree. So long as you have this, you'll be able to see us even when other humans cannot. And if you ever want to return here and stay forever, all you have to do is eat it." He dropped the unassuming acorn into my palm. I held it to my heart, unsure of what to say.

"Thank you."

"May the sun warm you, may the earth hold you, and may the stars guide you, my child," the old Magnusbach waved his wand/conductor's baton, and I gently fell asleep once more.

I woke up in my own bed. I sighed, looking around my crummy apartment. One of my cats was batting something around the floor. It was the acorn. I picked it up and put it in my jewelry box. I'd figure out a way to string it on a necklace of some kind so I could keep it with me, I decided. I put slippers on my icy cold feet and padded into the kitchen. My fiancee was there, sipping a cup of coffee.

31

"There's a package for you," he said.

"I'll check it out."

Sure enough, there was a gayly wrapped box sitting on our coffee table. It was addressed to me in elegant script, but there was no return address. I opened it.

"What is it?" My fiancee asked. I'm sure the strangled gurgles that were coming out of my throat must have sounded rather alarming.

I still couldn't speak coherently, so I pointed at the box instead. It was filled to the brim with shiny golden coins.

"Wow, are those real gold? And what are these markings? They look ancient. I bet that genuine coins like this would be worth thousands upon thousands of dollars," my fiancee noted. "How many are there? Looks like around three hundred or so. That many could be close to a million dollars, even."

I squeaked.

"What, you don't mean that these are real? I thought they were a prop from one of your shows..." he trailed off looking at me. I caught my breath and kissed him.

THERE WAS A NICHOLAS ONCE

"There was a Nicholas once, though he was not a saint." So my mother whispered to me as we huddled together under a rough woolen blanket. The wind howled outside our windows like a mad dog.

"This Nicholas had a full, well-kept beard and a splendid uniform. But when the people tried to reach him and beg for his help, his tin soldiers lined the bridges of the great city to keep them back..." She stopped the story here, her lips trembling.

I could see the rest of the story in the visions that clouded my eyes and made me see things that weren't there. There was a scuffle. The tin soldiers grew restless and frightened. The crowd didn't disperse but pressed against the barricades. Clouds of steam rose from pleading mouths, some singing hymns and praise, others shouting, angry. Orders came down, and the tin soldiers fired their guns. The hymns turned to screams, and the river ran with blood that stained not-saint Nicholas a deep red.

"Your father was there," my mother said, keening like a rusalka lost in the bone-cracking cold. He'd carried a Holy Icon. When the shooting started, he sought sanctuary in a nearby church. The icon he'd carried was riddled with bullets and splattered with blood. He took it as a sign, mother told me. He'd not had my gift of visions, but he knew a sign when he saw one, or at least he thought he did. He became a Red.

My father had a black beard that he kept immaculately trimmed, even as his cheeks grew gaunt and sallow. He shined his boots every day. The day they came for him, he wore his old coat, the one that still had bullet holes and bloodstains from the war. He let me help him shine his boots, since his hands shook so violently he was afraid he'd smudge the job. When I was done, he clasped my hand in his, as though he had something important to tell me. But when he opened his mouth, I saw his lips pull back into a death's grimace, and strips of blackened skin peeled off his face. In my hands his fingers burned red-hot, their skin cracked and bleeding. His mouth worked like a silent scream. Bile rose in my throat and I felt faint, but then the vision fled. There he was, my ordinary father, though his eyes were watery and bloodshot, and his hands trembled. He patted me on the shoulder.

"Go fetch some firewood," he said.

I did not tell him about my vision, but he may have known his fate anyway. I threw my arms around his bony chest and hugged him close to me before I left. He smelled of wet wool and cigarettes, though he not had smoked in years.

I did not see the men who took my father. The hill where the village boys gathered firewood was a long way from our building, which was likely the reason my father sent me there. He did not usually ask me to fetch the wood by myself, since the hill, which seemed quite ordinary to everyone else, was terrifying to me.

That day it did not seem so bad, not at first. Ancient trees, which normally reminded me wild crones and furtive creatures with long sharp fingers, now looked like an ordinary forest. Dreary clouds hung overhead, and the world seemed as grey and desolate as a concrete bunker. I almost wished I could see them again, the gnarled wood-witches and leshies of my visions, or perhaps my imagination. Instead I gathered sticks and wood under winter-deadened trees weighted down by a heavy coat of frost. Branches groaned under layers of ice, then shuddered and cracked. The sound of them falling was muffled by the carpet of snow. The cracks made me think of gun shots. I imagined men pointing their guns at my father while his hands floated helplessly around him.

When they came for Nicholas, not the saint, he gave his daughters rich gifts to protect them--girdles sewn with diamonds, strong enough to stop bullets. I heard soldiers laughing at him, a tall, gangly man, and pushing him off his bike, leering at his beautiful daughters. Did he know that all was lost forever, or did he have some hope even then? Did my father know? Does anyone remember, after the bullets shatter their skulls, is there some soul or memory left, or are they as cold and dead as the winter trees?

When I came home with the wood the building was cold and dark, the windows as black as mourning. I felt my way up the uneven staircase, the dull thud of my feet the only noise. I found mother huddled on the bed. I couldn't see her, but I felt her face beneath my fingertips, chilled and wet with tears. There were no stories that night.

The next morning my mother had a gaping hole in her mouth where several of her teeth had been. I helped her wash the blood off her face. When I gingerly put a finger in her mouth to pry loose a jagged fragment of tooth, it was as though I felt along the edge of a great abyss, and I saw us falling, and my mother laughing madly because if she stopped laughing the screams would come and then they would never stop.

Nicholas had never known starvation. He and his family had eaten the finest, softest bread, the sweetest cakes, luscious fruits without a single flaw. His meat was so tender it melted on his tongue, like the flakes of snow I catch in my mouth when I grow hungry. More than hungry. My mother's clothes hung from her skeletal frame, and though her bruises faded, her skin had a sickly pallor. My babushka--my grandmother--came to care for us. She made thin gruel with the last of the provisions we'd been rationed and spooned it into my mother's broken mouth.

"Go fetch more firewood," she said to me. "Or we'll all freeze to death."

The hill no longer frightened me. I felt at home among the dark and tangled things. Wraith-pale, my heart as black and gnarled as a wood witch's fingers. Hidden creatures moved and groaned within their favorite trees, the old things of the earth, half asleep under the snow. I laughed and danced on the crags of their ancient home, wild and mad, I no longer knew which. And when I grew so hungry, I could no longer dance, I feasted on strips of frozen flesh, dead mice I dug out of tree trunks, dead birds frozen on branches.

I brought the remains of a dead rabbit home. Babushka pursed her lips at the half-rotten meat, then threw it in the pot with the gruel.

Soldiers came for Nicholas and his family. They posed them together and told him they would take a family picture. When they announced the execution, he did not understand. "What?" he said, "What?" They shot him in the chest. Perhaps this was a kindness. He did not have to watch his children die. Nicholas the Bloody, red blood spreading across his chest.

"He denounced us," my mother whispered. I lay in bed with my eyes closed, listening. "Commander Yakov as good as murdered my husband with his own hands."

"And now he is in command of rationing. There is no other way." Babushka's voice rasped, and she sounded as old as the forest. As frozen. "He is coming, whether you will or no. He told me that today while I stood in the bread line. Don't make him angry." A wrinkled hand stroked my hair.

In my dreams I saw Nicholas' ghost, his neat brown beard grown white as snow, a wild bramble of patchy hair. His eyes were filmy and red, and he howled like a cold wind through crooked branches, calling out for his lost children.

When I got home from school the next day, Commander Yakov was visiting my mother. Babushka sat outside the apartment door. She grasped my wrist.

"Don't go in yet," she said. "She'll let us know when it's time."

"Get some firewood?" I asked.

She nodded. "Your mother wouldn't want you here right now."

I turned to leave, then stopped. Sounds came from behind the door, grunting, then a terrible mewling, like the sound of a cat being drowned.

"Go!" grandmother hissed.

In the woods I saw Nicholas' four daughters, all beautiful in long white dresses, their skin as pale as fresh snow. They had survived the first bullets, protected by the diamond girdles their

37

father gave them. They tried to flee. The youngest reached the door, and the soldiers hesitated to butcher such an innocent. They half-heartedly stabbed at her with their bayonets, which bounced off her diamonds.

When I returned, my mother had bruises around her neck shaped like a man's fingers. She was washing red stains off of our blankets. But when she saw me, she tried to smile.

"Salt pork," she said. "Rye, barley, a few potatoes." She clamped a hand over her mouth, as though the thought of food made her ill.

We ate in silence. My stomach writhed and heaved as though I'd swallowed worms.

Nicholas' daughter did not escape. I wanted to believe she had, but the visions never lied. When the bayonets didn't work the commander pulled out his pistol and shot each of the girls in the head, twice. I saw them singing to each other, holding hands in the woods. They danced in a circle, but each step left a puddle of blood, and their song was as sad and haunting as the nightingale's lament.

Commander Yakov had a thick brown mustache in imitation of our glorious leader, but beneath it his teeth were yellowed and rotten. His breath stank like cheap vodka and his skin was sallow and flabby. I first met him at our New Year's celebration, since we could not celebrate Christmas anymore. He brought butter and fruit kompot. Babushka made blini. My mother sat beside him, her hands plucking at the loose threads of her dress. Her eyes were flat and blank and staring, like those of the dead.

"Eat," he told her, handing her a blini stuffed so thick with preserved fruit it dripped red juice. "Surely you've swallowed thicker things before!" He laughed and clapped his hand on her knee. His fat yellowed fingers looked like worms feeding on her corpse. She stiffened at his touch, then opened her mouth and chewed mechanically.

"And you, little comrade, are you going to ask Ded Moroz to bring you anything this year?" I tore my eyes away from where he was pinching my mother, leaving a trail of red-blue marks on her skin.

"Ded Moroz?" I asked.

"The Old Man of Winter. He's the kindly Grandfather Frost and brings gifts to good children." He smirked at me, as if he was telling me a good joke I was too stupid to understand.

No grandfather would ever bring me what I truly wanted. "I don't think so," I said, my voice quiet and creaky from lack of use.

"What, what? You don't want to properly celebrate the holiday, as decreed by our Great Leader?" He loomed over me, and his smirk made me shudder. My mother squirmed uncomfortably, swallowing a piece of blini.

"Yakov," she whispered, "Leave her be. She's too old for such things."

"She'll soon be old enough for others, though," he said. He took off his belt and snapped it in his hands. My mother shuddered. "It's better she has a beating now than a bullet later, don't you think? You don't want her to end up like her father." He smiled at that and squeezed her breast with a pasty hand. She winced.

Nicholas never beat his children. His son would have been too delicate to withstand such rough treatment. He had fragile skin that bloomed with bruises from the lightest touch, so his parents doted on him, protected him. But when I saw him in my visions, his face was grave with sorrow. He was thirteen years old.

Yakov dragged me into the snow behind the coal bins. He pushed me down over a coal bin and unzipped his pants. A cold, sinking feeling settled in the pit of my stomach, but he only took a piss on the coals near my head. The stink of his urine filled me with rage, but I don't move. Even if I could kill him, what good would it do? They'd send me to the gulag, and maybe mother and babushka too. My face and hands went numb with cold, and I let the chill numbness spread over the rest of my body. His blows didn't bother me, even when my blood splattered against the snow. I felt nothing.

My mother found me out in the snow. She wrapped me in our blanket and pressed her lips to my cheek.

"I know you hate him," she whispered. "Maybe you hate me too. That's fine. Hold on to your hate. Ball it up inside you and feed it every day. It will keep you alive."

She carried me inside. Commander Yakov was gone, but he had forgotten to take the kompot with him. My babushka made me a blini, soaked in butter and filled with red fruit. As I ate the numbness wore off, and tears pricked my eyes. I wiped them away with the back of my fist. Then I gritted my teeth and compressed the pain into a squirming ball of hate in my guts.

Nicholas was weak. He loved his children, but he could not save them. The mad monk, the wild man whose dark charisma made him seem demonic to his enemies, was the only one who helped Nicholas' son. Innocence was a lie, a trick adults played on children to keep them under control. Nicholas' children were good. Good children who had died in the wars their elders waged. Good children who'd waited, patient and silent, while the lives they'd been promised melted away like last winter's snows.

Saints and Curses

I would not be good. I would turn away from the sad, lost ghosts that had haunted me so long. What could Nicholas offer me, when he let his own daughters die? I honed my hate until it was a sharp as a headsman's ax.

By Christmas eve, a few days after the Russian New Year, my hate had grown strong enough that I felt the dark power of the earth moving in my blood. The half-healed welts on my back itched and throbbed, keeping me wide awake even as my mother and grandmother nodded off. I waited until the moon rose, then slipped into the night.

The hill was shadowed and dark. The fine coat of crystalline snow had fallen that evening, but the pure white only made the shadows seem darker. The whispers in my blood pulled me to an ancient tree, gnarled and twisted in the moonlight. It was surrounded by a thick bramble, as black and wild as a madman's beard. I could not remember seeing it before, though its trunk rose from the frozen ground like a colossus. Fear curdled in my belly, but I clenched my hands into fists and came closer.

Branches caught on my clothes like fingers. They twined around me, ice cold. I felt them scrape against the half-healed welts along my back, until my blood splattered the snow and dripped from black twigs. I made a guttural sound and fought the urge to pull away.

"Help me," I said, my voice low and hoarse. Hate throbbed in my veins. The branches loosened but kept me caught in their grasp.

Thick limbs curled away from the ancient tree's trunk like goat horns, and I heard a voice in my head as cold and ancient as the frozen earth. It spoke a language that tickled

41

my memory like a half-forgotten dream, but I understood its question well enough.

"Death," I said. "For the commander of the Garrison, Yakov."

Bramble tendrils licked at the blood on my back, gentle now, but I shivered all the same. The voice spoke again, like cracking ice and groaning wood.

"Anything," I said. "Whatever you want."

I did not hear its voice so much as feel its desire, deep and old and hungry, and only the sharp edge of my hate kept me from quaking in fear.

"Can you protect my mother?" I asked. "Will you make him suffer?"

The ground rumbled and shook, as though with cold laughter. It let me go, and though my knees wobbled, I did not fall.

I knelt before the tree. Cold air bit my skin with a thousand pin pricks, but I took off my jacket, offering my blood to the hungry branches. I scratched my palm against a sharp root, then pressed the quivering, bleeding flesh to the black bark. My lips formed a sacred oath.

I felt the branches entwining me even before I was done. A gap opened in the trunk, a split I had not seen before, and it swallowed me whole, stuffing me into the cold earth like meat in a sack. The gap in the tree closed after me, and I was alone in the dark, except for my visions.

I saw Commander Yakov stumbling home, drunk. He hummed a revolutionary anthem to himself and leaned against a tree. Then, though there was no wind and the tree seemed young and healthy, it gave a sickening lurch. The commander looked up, dazed. Perhaps if he had been sober, he might have escaped in time, but he was not. He scrambled backwards and tripped, and the tree fell on top of him with a satisfying crunch. He screamed for help and pushed helplessly against the weight that pinned him down. He struggled. I watched as his cries grew weaker, as soft sobs became desperate mewling. As trails of blood spread out against the snow.

When at last his eyes closed and his breath grew still, I opened my eyes again. It was not dark any longer, or else my eyes had adjusted to lack of light. And I had changed. Green tendrils sprouted from my fingertips like crocus buds pushing up through the snow in spring. My skin had hardened into a tough grey bark. I stroked the wood of my prison, and the tree opened for me. But when I stepped into the dawn, my feet rooted themselves to the forest floor.

Now, it's not so bad, not really. Lost children come here and play near my roots. Nicholas' daughters come to visit me, too, dancing in circles, their laughter like the cries of birds. I saw my mother once. She came to the forest and called my name, over and over. When she grew tired, she sat down beneath my branches and buried her head in her hands. I tried to speak to her, but my voice was the rustle of leaves in the breeze. She looked up, puzzled, then shook her head. I have not seen her since.

I have not seen Nicolas either, nor the elder tree with its dark power. When the icicles melted and fresh leaves sprouted from dark branches, the elder tree's strength waned. But winter will return again, and when it does, I will ask the ancient tree to teach me the magic of wild things. Then I will step out of my tree on moonless nights and frolic under the light of the stars. And when lost children cry beneath my branches, I'll help them as the tree helped me.

Lantgen

SNAKE EYES

"They work miracles, Jodin!" Kella's eyes, or rather her one good eye, swept mine, pleading. "My God-Aunt took me to one of their ceremonies last night. They heal people, make old people young again, make injured people w-w-w-whole." Her voice trembled and rasped through the last sentence.

"I don't trust them," I said, gently patting her left hand, the one that's still smooth and soft, a trace of her former beauty.

Her shoulders twitched, and her veil wafted away from her face as she let out a heavy breath. Her left eye, the one that's green and gold like sunrise in a forest, filled with tears. The other eye stared ahead of her like always, red and black and full of pain, a mad eye. Both eyes looked at me now, one sobbing and the other burning.

"Ten years, I have lived like this, a curse. Ten years, and I didn't think I could bear it a single day." Kella's hands shook as she gripped her veil. My stomach dropped when I understood what she was doing. She lifted the richly embroidered purple cloth away from her face, something she had not done in the

45

past eight years. Not since the last healer said there was nothing else she could do.

She threw the veil to her feet, then unlaced the front of her robe as well. It fell to the floor, and she stood naked in the center of the room.

I forced myself not to gasp, or turn away, or otherwise show my discomfort. I knew my wife's body by touch, at least somewhat. I had run my fingers over her skin, the smooth and the scarred, and kissed the soft dimples that still remained on the left side of her neck. I had made love to her. But only on the darkest nights, and infrequently. I could not bear to admit to her, or even to myself, how much fear and revulsion I felt when I saw her.

I kept my gaze level and my features controlled. Thankfully, the room was dim and shadowy enough to conceal the worst of her disfigurement. "It's no worse than it was before, Kella. You are still my wife, and I love you."

Kella's mad eye blazed at me, and the left side of her face crumpled. The scars didn't move though; half her face was frozen forever in a terrifying grimace. At last she looked away. She fell to her knees, tears streaming from her green-gold eye as she groped for her clothes on the floor. Her breath came in choking, heaving rasps.

I bent down and covered her with her robe. She clung to the thick velvet cloth with her soft hand, its creamy white flesh blotchy from where she'd wiped away the salty tears. She grabbed my wrist with her other hand, the one with dried crackling skin. The fingernails on that hand had peeled off and never returned, but her skeletal fingers dug deeply into my flesh. My stomach twisted.

"You would deny me this?" Her voice hissed with bitterness.

I swallowed. "You don't know if it's safe, or if it even works. They could be lying to you, putting on a show."

"They are not. It's true what they say. Everything they do is real. I saw it with my own eyes."

I shifted my feet. "What about the cost?"

"I'd pay in service to the temple. It is not onerous."

"Kella..."

"It's a respected temple, Jodin. The Mother Serpent is worshipped and acknowledged throughout the lands to the east."

"But there have been rumors..."

Her grip on my hand tightened. "Would you deny me a cure because of a street-hag's gossip?" Her voice was soft and poisonous.

Shame pierced my heart. I wondered if she knew about the other girls, the giggling ones I met in quiet inns somedays. I had dreamed of her, had worshipped her, had never lusted for another woman's beauties. My mad desire had been for her. But that was a long time ago, and she knew it. Now I cared for her, loved her even, but my body did not desire her the way it had before the attack. Looking at her now, I could see so many traces of the luminous beauty she'd possessed then. But the traces were not enough to stir my lust. My shoulders slumped.

"It will be as you wish. We shall go the temple at moonrise."

She smiled then, and I wished I could have found her smile beautiful. But her lips pulled the mask of reddish scars into a puckered, ghoulish grin. I swallowed the bile that rose unbidden in my stomach and kept my face immobile.

That night we went to the Serpent's Temple. We had not gone anywhere together in years. Once, I'd coaxed and cajoled

47

her to come with me to the Maiden's Temple to receive her woman's blessing. I'd hoped it would give her comfort. It didn't. I remembered her shame and terror, and the fear in people's eyes when they saw her face. I'd thought that it would do her good to go out again, but it only convinced her a normal life was impossible. I hated all the people who'd stared at her or looked away. I hated myself more because I understood what they felt, all too well.

Now Kella pulled me through a thick crowd of people who stood in front of the Temple wearing ornate serpent masks. Our own masks were rather plain and inconspicuous, made of heavy black wood, primitively carved. Others had elaborate concoctions of silk with golden scales and vivid jeweled eyes. Yet Kella carried herself with such determined energy that the gold masks parted before us. A thousand masked eyes reflected the torchlight in a way that made me uneasy.

We watched the procession as it approached the Serpent Mother's gates, where the two stone cobras rose out of the earth twenty feet high. Two men beat heavy drums on either side of the gates. A line of priestesses stood before the cobra statues, golden snakes twining around their outstretched arms. Their masks were not the richest ones, but their vivid green scales moved in rhythm with the priestesses' strange dance, making them uncannily lifelike. Kella clutched my hand, and I felt her shiver as the high priestess approached the crowd. Her snake mask had brilliant orange fire-gems for eyes, and they glittered as she surveyed the crowd. She raised her hands. The drums stopped, and the priestesses flowed out into the crowd, their masks still undulating.

"What's happening?" I asked Kella. A sense of foreboding pierced me, and I wanted to cling to my poor, maimed wife. I drew her close to me. I imagined her face as it was before, hiding beneath her heavy wooden mask.

"It is the choosing," she said. "Not all may enter, only those who prove worthy..." Her words caught in her throat, and I felt her vibrating with hope and breathless anticipation. If the priestesses passed her by, she'd be crushed. I felt torn. My heart throbbed with the hope that they'd choose her, and she'd once more have the same smooth, delicate skin I'd dreamed of before our wedding. Yet some perverse part of me also hoped that they would ignore her. The snake women frightened me. I wanted us to go back home to our quiet life, where she'd be my broken angel forever.

A priestess with a piercing gaze sought us out. She had iron-grey hair trailing out from under her mask, and she stared directly at Kella, then at me. I squirmed beneath her hard glare. At last, she took Kella's hand, the burnt one, without one sign of hesitation or reluctance. I clung tightly to my wife's soft, pale hand as the priestess lead us through the Serpent gates. My pulse quickened as we passed beneath the stone cobras, their mouths yawning open to reveal marble fangs.

We followed the priestess down a narrow tunnel that twisted and wormed its way deep underground. When we at last stepped into the great hall, its brilliant lights and terrible splendor blinded me. We stood at the bottom of a circular arena, surrounded on all sides by a crowd of initiates in masks. Their seats reached to the top of the domed ceiling, and they stared down at us with icy jeweled eyes.

I shivered. "Are you sure?" I whispered to Kella, nuzzling her ear. She seemed to shrink, suddenly dizzy before all those eyes, and her body swayed. But she kept a fierce grip on my hand.

"I must."

The rest of the supplicants filed in behind us, some standing straight and proud, others bent over with age or sickness. One woman held a small, limp child in her arms. At last the high priestess entered the temple, not from the tunnel we'd passed through, but through a pinnacle on the roof. They lowered her in on a huge dais, and the drummers flanked on her either side. She raised her hands and the entire crowd rose to their feet. As one, they hissed like angry, spitting cobras.

I fell to my knees. "Please, Kella, don't do this!" I yelled, but my words were swallowed by the ferocious hissing crowd. I clung to her arms, pleading with my eyes and face. Her mad eye rolled in her head more violently than I'd ever seen it. She fixed her other eye on the priestess.

With a savage cutting motion, the high priestess silenced the crowd. She brought her fist to her chest, then swept it forward in a wide arc. At her gesture, the stone floor of the area shook beneath my feet. I tried to pull Kella back from the middle of the floor, where two enormous slabs of marble parted, revealing a huge pit filled with snakes. There were thousands of them, undulating against one another, hissing and twisting and spitting. I saw cobras, large and small, constrictors, every kind I knew and many more I didn't, in every color imaginable. And in the middle of this horrible pit, there rose a single, narrow pillar, wide enough for one person to stand on.

My heart stopped. "My love, you can't do this!" I begged Kella. Dizzy with fear, I clutched at her, my crumpled flower, my burnt angel. I promised I'd do better, I'd love her for who she was, I'd learn to cherish her scars. She looked at me unseeing. Or perhaps, I feared, seeing too much.

Saints and Curses

Hulking eunuchs emerged from the crowd carrying an enormous slab of marble. They positioned the marble to make a bridge across the pit, to the narrow pillar. The high priestess lowered her fist. A black-haired priestess led the first supplicant to the marble bridge. With trembling hands, the supplicant removed her mask and her robe, revealing herself to be an elderly woman. Naked and shivering, she hobbled out to the pillar. When she arrived, the eunuchs removed the marble slab. The old woman wrung her hands, and her knees shook so violently I feared she'd fall off the pillar. Seeing her there made me want to scream. I wanted to make the horrible ritual end and take my wife home.

The high priestess pointed her hands to the ground, and I watched, helpless, as the pillar sank beneath the old woman's feet, slowly lowering her into the pit of snakes. One by one, snakes slithered up the old woman's body and sank their fangs into her flesh. She gave a sharp scream as they entwined around her until they engulfed her completely. I felt faint as I watched the ball of serpents writhe. But moments later the pillar started to rise again, and the snakes released their victim. As the serpentine bodies fell away, I saw the old woman's body had changed. She stood straight and tall, and her legs no longer shook. Her hair, which had been salt white, turned chestnut brown. After the eunuchs set the marble bridge back in place, she walked with a steady gait back across the pit. The priestesses washed the blood and venom from her body. She stood before the crowded arena, no longer an old woman, but an exultant beauty in the first flush of youth.

Kella stared at the now-youthful woman, entranced. "It could be me next," she said, every word ringing with hope. I didn't reply. A tumult of emotions swirled inside my heart--fear, relief, amazement. I didn't know what to think anymore. I stared at the woman's eyes. For a moment, they glowed a poisonous yellow. I shuddered.

Kella wasn't next. Instead, a burly young man took his turn. He smirked as he sank into the snake pit, eyeing us with contempt. It took me a while to realize something had gone wrong. The snakes had engulfed him, and bitten him, just as they had the woman before. But he did not stop screaming for a long time, and his shrieks grew wilder and more desperate. I saw him thrashing around, his hands frantically tearing at the snakes as they surrounded him. When at last the pillar rose again, only his skull and a few odd bones were left. They had been picked clean. The crowd hissed. My heart pounded in my ears.

The sharp-eyed priestess tugged at Kella's hand. "You're next," she said, her voice flat and cold. Kella nodded and started to go with her.

"No!" I screamed. I refused to let go of her hand, her beautiful hand. "Kella, listen to me. It's too dangerous! You can't risk it!"

Kella turned towards me, her eyes blazing. She shoved me away from her. One of the eunuchs approached us. With blinding speed, he gripped my wrist and turned it, forcing me to let Kella go. I called after her, babbling my promises again.

The sharp-eyed priestess fixed me with a contemptuous glare. "Are you moaning because you love her, or because you're ashamed to admit you don't love her?"

Shame burned inside my stomach like a strong acid. "She's my wife," I said.

"You stayed with her after your wedding, of course. But did you treat her like anything other than a secret burden? Did you keep faith with her?" The priestess gave me a mocking smile.

"Tell me honestly, if she dies in the serpent pit, will you be more relieved than sad?"

I choked on my words. "No, it's not...I didn't mean..." Then my shoulders slumped. I watched as they lead Kella away.

They took her to the marble bridge. Hushed silence fell over the crowd. I heard her sobbing as she removed her robe with shaky hands, as she had earlier today, exposing her scarred flesh to the harsh light of the arena. When she removed her mask, I heard a few gasps. The hideous scars that covered her face and body left her looking monstrous, barely human. Staring at her now in the bright lights, I wondered how I could ever love someone like that. How could she be a real wife to me?

Kella crossed the marble bridge unsteadily. She'd always hated people staring at her; the crowd must've felt unbearable. She stood naked on the pillar, all her scars, all her pain visible to anyone who wished to see.

I looked away. I heard a slight rumble and knew that she was sinking into the pit of snakes. I heard her scream and knew they tore at her tortured flesh, bit her with their venomous fangs. I covered my ears.

The people around me stirred, and only then did I look up. Kella rose from the pit. Her hair, which had fallen out where the acid burned her skull, grew once more in luxurious red and gold waves. When they washed away the blood and venom, her skin was as whole and white and luminous as it had been the day we'd first met. Her arms and legs, which had been frozen in stiff, unnatural positions, were as supple and youthful as fresh willow branches. Her beauty ravished me, and the passions and longing I had once felt for her roared to life. I loved her, with the exquisite aching glory that comes with first love.

She faced me, and I saw her eyes. Not her mad burnt eye, not her sad green and gold eye, but cold, poisonous yellow eyes. I stepped back. Kella was lovely beyond compare, and I'd never lusted for her so desperately. But one look from those cold eyes, and I knew.

I'd never have her again.

SWITCHED

Blood-tinged water gushed from between my legs as I hobbled into the hospital. My contractions came fast and hard, so quick I knew no one in my family would make it in time for the birth. My poor husband Tom was in a different hospital somewhere in Afghanistan. The last I'd heard from the military he was touch and go; I feared this baby would be the last thing I'd have of him. A spasm tore its way across my belly, and hospital staff surrounded me. They wheeled me down a long, eerily quiet corridor. Nurses whispered to each other, exchanging odd looks. I felt alone, except for the primal blood connection that linked me to my infant.

Things started going wrong, and the doctor muttered with concern. C-section, he told me, it's the only way. I gave my consent because I couldn't risk the precious being I carried. They wheeled me into an operating room and strapped my arms down. Numbed from the waist down, there was strong pressure on my abdomen as the doctor pulled the baby out of my womb. I wept to hear her cry.

"Bring her to me," I begged. "I need to see my baby."

A nurse carried her over, and I held her, memorizing every contour of her precious face and warm, wet body. Beautiful, sweet little girl. Then a doctor I hadn't seen before appeared out of nowhere, smiling sardonically. Something about him seemed wrong...off. Were his eyes red? Was I just seeing things? Before I could say anything, he shoved a needle in my IV, and I lost consciousness.

I woke up in the recovery room, groggy. I trembled, freezing cold, and anxious for a nurse. I wanted my baby with me, my new little girl. I'd call her Fiona, after my grandmother. Looking around, I saw I was alone--no nurses, no bassinet for the baby. I hit the call button on my bed. A chirpy voice answered. "Yes? Is there something you need?"

"Could someone bring me my baby? I'd like to try to nurse her right away." They'd recommended that at the parenting classes I had attended before my delivery.

"Hold on." There was a long pause. "Oooh, I'm afraid there've been some complications...it'll be just few more minutes..."

"Complications?" For a second, I couldn't breathe. Time seemed to stretch endlessly, until at last I heard the squeaking wheels of a hospital cart approaching my bed. A nurse pushed an incubator into the room. She reached out to hold my hand. My arm hung awkwardly in her grasp, as limp and cold as a dead fish.

"Before I give you the baby, I just want you to be prepared...it seems the child suffers from some kind of metabolic disorder. We've called in a specialist to identify it, but he seems stable enough for now, so I don't see any reason why you can't try to nurse it...I mean, him."

"Him? My baby is a girl. They saw that on the ultrasounds."

56

The nurse looked over her clipboard. "Nope, must have been a mistake. It shows here that the baby is a boy." She lifted the baby from its incubator, holding it at arm's length before depositing it on my chest.

I pulled back the swaddle that covered the child's face, then froze in shock.

The first thing I noticed were the menacing blood-red eyes. Its skin was leathery and dingy grey, more like the wings of a bat than the tender pink baby skin I remembered. The fingers that stretched out beneath the blanket ended in claw-like nails. Its mouth yawned open, revealing a row of razor-sharp teeth.

"What is this thing? That's not my baby. Is this some kind of a joke? I had a beautiful little girl. I saw her--I was going to call her Fiona. This isn't even human. Where is my baby? My real baby? Where's my Fiona?"

"There, there, I know it's a shock. It's not what any mother expects, but sometimes things go wrong in the delivery...genetic problems...maybe exposure to toxic chemicals..." The nurse patted my hand, her voice full of the obnoxious perkiness I associate with salespeople and cheerleaders.

"NO, this isn't real--that's not my baby. Where is my real baby? My sweet Fiona? This is an abomination!"

"Just try to relax and accept it. Maybe once you've held him for awhile, you'll feel more bonded." A bland smile crept across the nurse's face as she spoke. Was I seeing things? Did her eyes flash red? Sweat trickled down my face.

"Maybe you should try nursing him?" she chirped.

"No, no, no, this is not right. Please take it away." The creature writhed in my arms, unnaturally strong. It raked its nails across the skin of my chest. I winced.

The nurse murmured something about "post-partum psychosis" and "many new mothers suffering" then "you'll feel better when you feed him."

"I don't want that thing near me!" I pleaded anxiously. But an iron grip clamped my hand, and to my horror the nurse shoved the foul thing towards my breast, pushing aside my hospital robe. The creature clamped its teeth down on my nipple, sending agonizing pain radiating through my body. It sucked greedily, drinking my oozing blood instead of milk. I screamed, and blackness took me.

I had vague sensations of people moving around me, pulling my body onto a bed in a private room, removing the epidural from my back, and taking out my IV. Through it all, I mumbled incoherently about my stolen infant, my sweet Fiona. Few listened to me and none believed that she was gone. They patted me sympathetically and whispered to each other "hysterical" or "bad reaction to the drugs." I knew no one here would help me find her. Terror froze my insides. Trapped in my own body, I could barely move my legs.

At last I felt my full consciousness returning. My legs felt heavy and numb from the epidural, but I could move them, however weakly. I wanted my beloved baby Fiona so intensely I felt as though I'd lost a limb or a part of my body I hadn't realized I had. Who took her, and why had they replaced her with that abomination?

I remembered the old stories I'd heard from my grandmother. Fairies, sometimes called the People of Peace, would steal human children away, leaving one of their own behind. To get her baby back, a mother had to throw the changeling into the fire or kill it somehow. I shuddered. I didn't want to throw any child into a fire, even a demonic one. And those were just stories, right? They couldn't be real. But I had to find my baby, and the only clue I had was the monster that had been left in her place.

I took a shaky breath and called for a nurse. Thank God, the nurse who came wasn't the one from the night before.

"Grisella only works nights," the new nurse told me when I asked about the other nurse. I told her to bring me the baby.

I hoped and prayed that maybe I'd dreamed the whole thing, that this new, more human nurse might bring me a human baby. But that was not to be. In the daylight, the creature looked even less human, its features twisted and its skin as wrinkled as dried leaves. At least its eyes stayed half-closed, as though it was sleepy or didn't like the light.

When the nurse left, I examined the creature further, from its gnarled feet to the matted black hair on its head. I took off its diaper. It was male, all right, but worse, it had a scaly little snake tail that curled out of the base of its spine. I shuddered to touch it.

I couldn't burn this demon-spawn--I didn't have any matches or fuel. But I could find another way to bring my precious human infant back. There was a bathtub in my bathroom. Maybe demons hate water, too...

But what if it didn't work? What if I was wrong? Maybe the whisperers were right, maybe I'd gone insane...

The spawn writhed in my arms. It grinned, revealing razor sharp teeth. My breast still throbbed where it had bitten me.

"What are you? Why are you here? Where is my real baby?" I asked. My voice cracked. It only laughed back at me, a malevolent gleam in its eye.

"Please, I can't let anything bad happen to her. Is she safe? Will they hurt her?" The creature stuck out a long, forked tongue. It licked its lips, hungry. I felt sick.

"Bring her back to me. I'll do anything." Tears ran down my face. The changeling laughed again, a horrible sound like rusty gears grinding together.

My body was still so helpless. My insides burned like a roaring fire when I pushed myself to sit up in bed. Standing up was so excruciating my vision blurred and I thought I might faint. I forced myself to pick up the vile spawn and carry it towards the bathroom. Every step I took made me feel like my incision might rip open. The creature started thrashing in my arms. It howled like a demented wolf and dug its claws into my body, tearing deep gashes. But I held on. I couldn't let it get away until it brought back my real child.

In the bathroom, I fell on my knees before the tub and filled it with icy water, careful to keep one hand clenched on the creature's leg so it wouldn't escape. It growled at me and bit my hand. When the tub was full, I clenched my fists around the spawn's legs and forced it into the water with what little strength I possessed. It writhed in my hands. When its withered body went limp, I pulled it out.

"Bring me my baby," I whispered, too weak to yell. It snapped back to life and hissed at me, baring its teeth. I pushed it back underwater, praying that it would give up. This time, I could barely hold it. I clutched its kicking legs as it thrashed violently, until I could feel the wound in my abdomen tearing open. I fought to keep from blacking out. As I blinked, I saw that the creature had started to melt away, its skin disintegrating into a sticky black tar.

"NO!" I screamed. "Bring her back, demon! Bring her back!" I sank my hands through the foul black ooze, but I couldn't feel the bottom of the tub--it was as though my hands had reached into some void, a dark hole in the world. Was it my imagination, or did I feel a tiny hand somewhere in there?

I grasped the small, warm hand and pulled, gently now. I felt a connection surging through me. Out of the blackness and icy water, I pulled that warm little hand until it emerged from the tub, and I saw her arm, her sweet face, her soft, newborn body. I heard her cry and pressed her to my chest. I kissed her face.

Blood poured from the gash in my belly and mixed with the cold water and foul, black sludge. Pain darkened my vision, but I fought to stay awake, feasting my eyes on my own, my beloved, my baby. I slumped to the floor, arms still wrapped around my child, sweet Fiona. My baby sighed and nuzzled against my skin. The pool of red around us grew larger. I closed my eyes. I'd never been so happy.

Lantgen

CINNAMON ULTRA PUMPKINATOR

I twirl and bow as a bevy of customers stomp into the coffee shop, though most of them have the grumpy look of people who just got done working terrible jobs. I fluff up the orange and red skirt I'm wearing as part of my "fall fairy costume." Time to spread joy! I pick up my tray filled with samples of our specialty fall latte--Cinnamon Ultra Pumpkinator--and offer them around, being sure to shower each customer with "magic" from my spice wand.

Hmm, well, no one seems to be embracing the fall spirit! Why several even cringed when my wand sprinkled them with glittery fall-themed confetti, and no one took any of my samples! I sigh with frustration.

"Sales have been down," Brad, my weird and sort of creep manager, had told me. "And they want us to get rid of all the fall stock before Christmas hits. We need to spice it up a bit!"

Of course sales are down, I think. I'm not allowed to drink it anymore, and clearly other people don't have as much fall spirit as I do. Cinnamon Ultra Pumpkinator is to fall flavors what ghost peppers are to salsa. One cup is enough to set my pulse

63

racing and make my mouth taste like cinnamon and nutmeg for the rest of the day. No one drinks it but the most dedicated pumpkin spice buffs, and even most of us consider it the hard stuff.

I am, of course, the queen of the pumpkin spice fans. Literally. I was elected "Pumpkin Spice Queen" by the fan website I ran. Until recently that is, when that awful Regina Simmons stole my crown while simpering about supporting my "recovery." But just because my court-appointed therapist will no longer allow me to drink the delicious elixir after the "incident" doesn't mean I can't appreciate the perfection of a good Pumpkinator!

Personally, I think it's really unfair. How does one little psychotic break get me banned from consuming Pumpkinators for life? I don't even remember most of what happened that one time, and I'm sure it's an isolated incident caused by stress or something, not "an intense chemical dependency on the combination of cinnamon, nutmeg, and caffeine," like that stupid judge said.

Well, my therapist, Dr. Beverly Kasowitz, can't keep me from having a job, although Bev did give me serious frowny face when I told her about the job at CaffeineFreek.

"Isn't that where they make those drinks, the ones that--"

"Don't worry, Bev, they make many fine beverages there, including many that are caffeine-free to appeal to the health conscious," I told her, smiling as meekly as I could. "And the Cinnamon Ultra Pumpkinator won't be around much longer. Everyone knows they'll be releasing their new winter drinks super early this year."

"But--" Bev had persisted. She meant well, I'm sure, but she's one of those mousy-haired women who look perpetually startled. I've no idea how she got her current job, which must involve talking to people way more messed up than me.

"Anyway, I super pinky promise I won't go near the pumpkinators. And this way I can be responsible and save for college and ummm...it's the only job I can find that, umm, offers health insurance." Which was true, and when you have a history of mental breakdowns involving hospitalizations, is a point of consideration.

Bev would freak if she saw me now, wearing golden tights, a glittery orange and red tutu, and a leotard festooned with fall leaves and pumpkin paraphernalia. And of course, I'm also holding an entire tray of Cinnamon Ultra Pumpkinator samples. Their smell makes my mouth water. I remember that sweet, sweet burn of strong cinnamon and hot coffee, the way it slid down my throat and warmed my belly. And right here are some stupid customers walking right by me without drinking a delicious sample. I wave my spice wand again, but the customers duck away and still no one takes a cup.

The worst part is, what I do remember of the incident--my notorious pumpkin spice-induced breakdown--is having the best night of my life. The scent of rich, spicy goodness from the samples dredges up vague memories of crisp, magical fall colors. And I mean truly *magical*--the volunteer firefighter that got me down from the old oak tree in my best friend's yard swore I was ranting about elves.

I'd like to know if I said anything more, but I don't know how to contact him (I never got a name, but apparently called him "the long-lost prince of Angemere" all night). And my best friend Monica, or should I say former best friend, refuses to talk to me! Even after I apologized profusely for what happened to her cat! I even pointed out that Nibbles wasn't injured or likely to be permanently affected in any way, but she was still furious.

Sigh. And now my former best friend won't get to see me glammed up in my glorious "fall elf" costume. Though she did hate CaffeineFreek, even before the incident. I can just imagine the way she'd arch her eyebrows and say something devastating if she could see me now, something like--

"Are those glittery acorns on your butt?"

Of course. Most people have to speak of the devil, but I just have to think about a person I'd rather not see, and they appear as if by magic.

"No. If you must know, those are supposed to be the magical nutmeg seeds that give Cinnamon Ultra Pumpkinator its special—lusciousness."

"That's not nutmeg," Monica says in that dry know-it-all voice of hers.

"How would you even know?"

"I've been studying botany. I'm thinking about expanding my garden next year, and I got a new job in a greenhouse after school."

"Oh." Monica did love plants. She's one of those weird people who talks to trees and animals as if they can understand what she's saying and talk back. And she has the nerve to tell me I'm the crazy one!

"So why are you here?" I ask. "Not to admire my costume, I take it." I swirl.

"No," she says with a hint of sarcasm. "Though I'll admit that's a nice perk. There's something I need you to see, right away. What time do you get off work?"

I glance down at my tray of luscious samples. I had considered taking a few brief sips once my shift ended, but

Monica would smell the cinnamon on my breath. I could tell her I was busy after work, but she knows when I'm lying like she possesses a magic power to see inside my brain. In fact, she's no doubt reading me right now, so she already knows everything I'm thinking. Oh my god, I need to think fast to come up with a good reason or else--

"So, I'm guessing around eight? Great, I'll pick you up."

"But I'm...umm...going someplace..." God, I need to get better at coming up with excuses. If I wasn't afraid of spilling my samples I would facepalm right now.

Monica rolls her eyes. "I wouldn't ask if it wasn't important, Crystal. Besides, you should apologize to Nibbles. She still smells like cinnamon, and I've bathed her three times."

"Apologize to the cat! But--"

"Aren't you addicts supposed to apologize to everyone you've wronged? Isn't that one of the steps or something?"

"I'm not in a program like that, for your information, I just have a court-appointed therapist. But--" I sigh. I do miss Monica, and if I have to apologize to a cat, well, sometimes you have suck it up, buttercup. That's what my mom is always telling me in that exasperated tone of hers, the one she saves for my most glorious disasters. "Fine. I'll apologize to Nibbles, if it means that much to you."

"It does. Nibbles is special, you know, she's not an ordinary cat."

I refrain from commenting. I've never seen Nibbles do anything extraordinary besides stare at me as though she knows exactly what I'm thinking or what I'm about to do, and she totally disapproves. But at least ninety percent of cats have mastered that stare, so it's not special.

By the time my shift is over, I have a sticky film of glitter on my skin and I smell like coffee grounds and cinnamon. I can't wear my costume home, so I pull my favorite oversized sweatshirt over my head and slip on old jeans.

Monica is driving the notoriously terrible car she bought with her lifeguard money over the summer. The engine's so janky you can hear it coming a mile away, and it still smells like old pizza. I go to open the door, but Monica shakes her head and rolls down the passenger side window.

"The latch got stuck and now the door won't open. You have to climb in through the window."

"You've got to be kidding me."

"Nope."

Despite what they show on ancient TV shows, it is impossible to slide through a car window in any way that's cool or graceful. No, most people end up awkwardly stuffing themselves inside feeling like they somehow have too many limbs, and did I bump my head hard enough to cause a concussion?

Once inside, I grip the seat and pray Monica's driving has improved since the last time I was in a car with her. It hasn't, and I try not to be sick as she careens down the street.

I close my eyes. No, that makes it worse. I open them again and try to focus on why Monica is talking to me in the first place.

"So, what's this mysterious thing I need to see?" I ask.

"There's a message in the tree."

"What!? You haven't been umm, "talking" to the tree again, have you? Because I totally did not leave any messages on or in or with the tree. I haven't even been back there since that night, so--"

"It's not that like that. You kind of have to see it. Although it's sort of hard to see in the first place. I wouldn't have even noticed it, but Nibbles was sniffing it."

68

"Weird."

"Yeah."

I don't know what to say at this point, so I pull out my phone and pretend to send a text to someone, so I'll feel less awkward. Only, I suspect Monica knows I'm pretending, so now I feel more awkward than before. I wish I had some Cinnamon Ultra Pumpkinator right now. It always makes me feel so much better.

We finally pull up to Monica's yard and I struggle out of the car. It's a cool fall evening, and leaves crunch under my feet. The tree looms over us. It's the largest and oldest tree in the county, and Monica and I spent whole afternoons playing in its branches. But the growing darkness shades its orange-red leaves an ominous grey, and its long black limbs make me shiver.

Nibbles is outside, batting at leaves. She flounces up to Monica and rubs against her legs, purring. She glares at me with those witchy green cat-eyes.

"Look," I say to Nibbles. "It's not completely my fault, so I don't know why you're--"

Monica gives a loud "ahem!" and I sigh. Nibbles and I had gotten along okay after Monica rescued her from a dumpster when she was a tiny grey fluffball. And perhaps I did owe her an apology after the "incident," although considering how many scratches I had I seriously think she owes me one, too. I mean, I don't remember exactly what went down, but it's not like I wasn't trying to help. At least, I think I was.

"Nibbles," I begin, trying not to feel stupid, "I'm sorry, ummm, for throwing up on you. I seriously didn't mean too. I was just trying to get you down from the top of the tree. I don't know even know how either of us got up there in the first place, but I'm sure my intentions were pure."

69

"Wait," Monica says. "There's no way you climbed that tree to get Nibbles."

"Of course I did. Why else would I have climbed the tree in the first place?"

"You tell me. But I know for a fact that you were up there before Nibbles was. She was on my lap, then she freaked out like she does when there's a thunderstorm and ran outside. I followed her, then I heard a huge crash, and you were at the top of the tree. Nibbles climbed up towards you, and you vomited enough Cinnamon Ultra Pumpkinator on her to make her smell like pumpkin spice for over a month."

That last part was true. I'd caught a whiff of nutmeg when the cat rubbed on Monica.

"But that doesn't make any sense--"

"None of it makes sense," Monica said. She pointed at the tree. "Take a look. It's easiest to see when the moon's rising."

I looked. Letters were forming on the trunk of the tree, faint and silvery like starlight. I couldn't tell if the letters were growing out of the trunk somehow, or if the tree branches had shaped themselves to angle the light to make them. It was the most delicately beautiful thing I'd ever seen.

It read: "She who consumes the spice--" then there was some elegant scribbling. Then, "Hello? Human girl, are you there? Have you brought the secret ingredients? We've been waiting for--" more scribbling. Finally, "Crystalline one, you must bring back the magic they've stolen from us, or all is lost. The spice--" Then it broke off.

"So, ah, do think they--you know, whoever wrote this--do you think they're talking to me?" I asked. I felt chosen and special and panicky and oh my god what do they want me to do?

"Umm, yeah," Monica said. She gazed at the tree with the look of someone who wasn't quite sure how magical phenomena fit into her world view.

"So, what do I do now?" I asked, which I know sounds like a stupid question.

"I don't know. But I think we should start by trying to figure out exactly what happened that night you had your, umm, incident."

"Great!" I try to sound sarcastic, but I think I fail.

"Let's retrace your steps. What started the night off?"

"Chemistry test. I went to CaffeineFreek to study..."

It was one of those evenings, the kind you sometimes have in fall, where the weather's still warm but there's a cool breeze that gently stirs your hair. My classes still felt fresh and exciting, not dull or draggy, so I didn't even mind studying.

I got a table outside on the patio and bought myself a CUP. They'd only come out a week or so earlier, so I was still savoring the new flavor, mmm, warm and spicy and foamy. I ordered mine with extra whip cream, oh so good. My lab partner was late, so I just sipped my drink and gazed dreamily at the golden yellow leaves quietly rustling in a nearby tree, glancing just enough at my chem book to feel productive.

I got a text from my partner, who said she couldn't make it after all, she hoped I'd understand, blah blah blah. I was just about to head home when Jonathan Kitzman, the geeky-hot guy working the counter that day, brought me another Pumpkinator.

"It's on the house," he said, and his voice cracked just enough to be adorkable.

"Thank you!" I said. "This is so my favorite drink ever."

"I like them too," he said, blushing.

"Awesome! You know, I'm the president of the Cinnamon Ultra Pumpkinator online fan club." I said that really fast, before I'd considered the fact that being president of fan club devoted to a coffee flavor might make me look a little...crazy.

Jonathan smiled. "That's cool."

If Jonathan hadn't said that, I don't think I've have ordered all those Pumpkinators just to talk to him. My heart started racing after the third one, and honestly, everything got kind of blurry after that. I've been too scared to ask Jonathan how many Pumpkinators I drank, or talk to him at all, even though we kind of work together now. It's awkward.

"So that's what I remember," I tell Monica. "After a few more CUPs, I had this awesome dream where I was flying. It was cool and magical and amazing, then I woke up in a tree and vomited on a cat."

Monica raises her eyebrows. "What about since then? Anything strange happen?"

"Hmm, well, Brad, the manager at CaffeineFreek, has been totally freaking out. Something about sales and product standards and annoying business stuff. There's supposed to be a corporate inspection this week."

"I seriously doubt CaffeineFreek has anything to do with magical writing that's appearing on my tree. I was talking about strange magical things, like, I dunno, leprechauns?"

I roll my eyes. "Don't be silly, Monica. Leprechauns aren't real. And the message on the tree clearly mentions secret ingredients, which could totally be related to coffee. There are huge discussions on the spice forums about how to make a good pumpkinator at home. A lot of people have tried to make them, but no one's succeeded yet in figuring out the right blend."

"Glittery acorns!" Monica smacks her palm into her forehead. "There's no way some corporate stooge used actual magic in their newest coffee flavor, is there?"

"Well, they are very hush-hush about the recipe..."

"And you did somehow end up at the top of a tree..."

I lean against Monica's car, trying to think. "But it's crazy. There's no way. Magic doesn't--"

"Doesn't what? Leave silvery messages on trees? I don't think it's up to us to say what magic can or can't do."

"But..."

Monica sighs and her lips do that twisty thing they do which means she's thought of something but doesn't want to say it. "Look...there's a way we can test it."

She gives me a meaningful look.

I give her a confused shrug.

She sighs again. "We need a guinea pig. One of us can drink a bunch of Cinnamon Ultra Pumpkinators while the other one watches for any magical effects."

"Oh no," I say, shaking my head, even though a big part of me really, really wants too. "My therapist...the judge..."

"Caffeine gives me jitters, and who knows? Magic might not work the same on everyone--it might not work on me at all. If it is magic, at least we know it works on you."

I should probably protest more and say something noble about the path to recovery and my determination to fight my demons, but I don't. The thought of a warm cup of spicy deliciousness makes my mouth water. It's been so long. I twirl for joy.

"Okay, you can stop twirling now. Let's meet at CaffeineFreek tomorrow evening. I'm going to monitor your consumption and make notes of the drinks' effects." Monica pushes back her glasses.

"You're such a nerd," I say, but I give her a warm smile to let her know I mean it in an affectionate way.

"And you are nuttier than all the fruitcakes from Christmas, but I love you anyway," she says, and I know she means it in the best way possible.

"Whee! I can fly!"

"No, you can't, Oh My God, what are you doing!?"

"This is amazing!"

"Get down from there! You're going to crash!"

"Whee! Monica, let's go!"

"Oh My God, Crystal, put me down! We're going to die!"

"No, we're going to see the elves! They're real! Yay!"

"If you drop me, I will kill you!"

The tree is below me, but it's not just a tree anymore, its branches are opening, they swirl, and there's silvery light.

"There's where we're supposed to go! I'm so happy!"

"What are you--Oh No--pull up, pull up!"

I drive for the portal, slipping us through its misty edges. It's like dancing on a moonbeam. Until my feet land someplace hard, slip out from under me, and my butt smacks against the ground.

"Ouch!"

Monica groans, pulls her black hair away from her face, and throws up the microwave pizza rolls she ate before we left.

I move to help her clean up her face with one of the handy wet wipes I keep in my purse for just such occasions (since the "incident," anyway). But I get the uncanny feeling that I'm being watched. I look around, trying to focus through caffeine induced jitter-vision. I finally notice a little brown man who looks like he's made of living wood. He squints at me over a long nose.

"Crystalline one?" He asks. His voice sounds a bit like rustling leaves.

"Yes?" I say, since I'm pretty sure he's talking to me.

"You have returned! Have you found where they are keeping the sacred branch?"

"Ummm, what?"

He sighs. It sounds a lot like those groaning sounds trees sometimes make on a windy day. "Let us take you someplace quiet and safe, where you and your companion may rest and recover."

"Sure, I mean, that's cool."

"Yes, I'm sure we can find a place with a temperature to your liking."

"Huh? Uh, okay, sounds good."

"Can you walk?"

"Sort of. My butt hurts."

"Well, follow me."

Honestly, that's the last thing I remember until morning, or whenever it is I wake up. It's hard to tell time when you're inside a tree.

Anyhow, I wake up when I hear Monica and the elf talking. It smells like they're drinking or eating some delicious, spiced substance, like Cinnamon Ultra Pumpkinator but without the coffee or the milk or the sugar.

"Nay," the elf says. "It's not like that. Ye shall not cause the end of all things. But it is mighty irksome to have humans addled by magic dropping into our dwellings. If we'd known about the alchemical reactions between human coffee beans and our Gleanna nuts, we'd ne'er have allowed humans to take a cutting of the sacred branch."

"So why not just ask for them back?" Monica asks.

"We have! But Brad the Manager, Laird of Caffeine and Freek, is a terribly stubborn bugger. Worse, he has cleverly surrounded his domain with steel and cold iron, which we cannot abide. I suspect he must be enjoying the effects of the powerful magic, though he has yet to come crashing through the sacred tree."

"I always knew Brad was up to no good," I chime in. "He gives me the worst shifts, and he smells like musty gym socks."

"Well, well," the elf says. "The sleeper has awakened. I'd get ye some Gleanna toast, but I fear you'd float right up to the ceiling after your first bite."

"But it smells soooo good," I say. My tummy rumbles.

"Aye, well, you'll have to fly back soon enough. Might as well break your fast ere you go." He slices a large seed cake, spreads it with golden butter, then grates a bit of bright red nut on the top.

I take a bite. It's amazing, the best bread I've ever eaten, rich with spices and creamy butter. I start to feel warm and tingly. The wooden room seems to sparkle more than it did before, but my feet stay firmly on the ground. Okay, maybe not firmly-- wait, it seems I am floating, but only an inch or so off the ground.

"Hmmm," Monica says, staring critically at my feet, which resolutely stay in the air. "Does the magic effect everyone? I've eaten the same thing, and I haven't started floating around."

The elf shrugs. "Some people fly, some might develop other talents, some might not ever feel more than a tickle."

"This whole flying thing," I sigh. "It's just...so, so awesome. Can I keep it? I mean, if we get the magic thingys back, could I keep one? Or a few?"

The elf looks doubtful. "As a species," he says, "humans have always done a poor job of managing magic. Besides, would you be satisfied with just one or two, or would you keep wanting more and more? It's easy to get in over your head you know."

I flip in midair. Why do people always think "getting in over my head" is a bad thing?

Monica rolls her eyes at my antics. "I guess we should be going. Here's hoping my mom didn't notice I was gone all night."

I fall back down to the floor with a crash. "Oh my god, I didn't even think about that! Let's go!"

After several tries at flying home (which is way harder when I think about it too much), I manage to crash land us on the roof of Monica's house. It's still super early in the morning, so our plan is to sneak in through Monica's bedroom window and pretend we've been there all night having a sleepover. Luckily, my parents are out of town for the weekend at a meditation retreat "to reconnect and recenter their lives." My mom heavily implied they desperately needed it after my recent legal troubles.

"So... how are we going to find these magic thingys?" I ask, flopping down on Monica's bed.

She flops down next to me. "I was thinking--don't you have some corporate inspection thing going on this week?"

"Yeah, it's today."

"Is there any way you can switch around your shifts, so you'll be working then? I bet the corporate guys make Brad open the back office and the umm, I don't know, vaults? Safety deposit boxes? Does CaffineFreek have a vault?"

"No, but they have a locked fridge. Brad says it's to keep employees from sampling too much of the product, but it does seem suspicious now that I think about it. I mean, who locks up cinnamon/nutmeg syrup?" I say.

"A locked fridge...wait, the elf said that Brad kept the Gleanna nuts surrounded by steel and cold iron. Could he have been talking about a refrigerator?"

"Well, he did say cold iron, and a fridge is cold--"

"We have to get inside that fridge!"

I came early for my shift and snuck Monica in the back door. I put on my fall fairy costume and gave her my regular uniform to change into, so that we both could blend in. At least, as well as I could blend in with a sparkly orange tutu and crinkly autumn leaves in my hair.

There were no corporate guys in sight yet, but Brad kept mopping sweat off his face with the napkins. Monica grabbed a cleaning rag and started wiping down tables. He didn't give her a second look.

The door snaps open and in walks a slim woman in a neatly tailored black suit with her hair pulled back in a tight bun. She's wearing sexy librarian glasses and her heels click authoritatively on the tile floor. She marches over to Brad, who sways on his feet as though he might faint.

"Whoa. Check out the killer corporate queen," Monica whispers.

"Do you think Brad is in love with her, terrified, or both?" I whisper back.

Before Monica has a chance to answer, the queen whips around at us.

"I see you are dressed as a fall fairy for our pumpkinator promotion. But where are your samples?"

Oh no, I forgot them! My mouth opens and closes so I look like an idiot fish, but somehow corporate queen's stare has paralyzed my vocal cords.

Brad jerks his head up. "Don't mind Crystal. She's only just arrived, and, umm, I wanted to make some of the extra special samples I've been telling you about."

"Yes, you have made some mention of the "special ingredient" you have found to enhance our Cinnamon Ultra Pumpkinator. But I am not pleased with unauthorized flavors being added to our products. You must understand, we have standards to uphold," the queen says in a clipped voice.

"If you could only try it," Brad says, smiling unctuously and dabbing sweat from his forehead. "It's going to be the next flat white! The next big trend, I'm telling you."

"Very well. If you insist, I shall try this...variant you have developed. If it is acceptable, then perhaps we can introduce it as an option at other franchises."

Brad sort of smiles again, but it comes out looking more like a leer. Monica snorts and rolls her eyes, but Brad and corporate queen don't notice.

They head to the back of the shop where the storeroom and the fridges are. Monica and I try to follow quietly, but Brad freezes us with a glare.

"Where do you two think you're going?" he sneers.

"Umm, samples?" I sputter. I sound like an idiot, and corporate queen gives me a pitying look, as though she's about to pat my head.

"Fine," Brad snaps. "But not her. I don't even remember hiring you," he says to Monica. "When did you start working here?"

Monica gives him her best exasperated sigh. "A week ago, when Jenna Jeffries quit," she says in a slow drawl as if she's had to remind him six times already.

Brad squint at her, then nods. "Those tables had better be spotless when we get back."

"Whatever you say, Brad," Monica says in a voice that sounds like a verbal eyeroll.

He looks like he's going to say something else to her, but corporate queen snaps her fingers and he comes running to her. I follow them into the back, trying to look meek and bland, which is hard to do when you're wearing a glittery orange tutu and covered in autumn leaves made of silk and sequins.

Nonetheless, Brad and the corporate queen barely afford me a glance. Brad is giving the corporate queen a simpering smile, and she's looking at him as though she's trying to figure out where a foul smell is coming from. Brad unlocks the "secret" fridge with what he no doubt thinks is an impressive flourish. I hold my breath. Here it is--what magical secret did Brad steal from the elves?

Brad opens the fridge, and I barely contain my disappointment. There's nothing in there that looks magical or impressive or amazing, just a sad glass jar with a wilted brown plant. My heart drops a little. Maybe I'm just crazy after all, like Bev the court-appointed shrink has been trying to tell me. Maybe I imagined the awesome incredible adventure and flying and elves. I nearly turn and walk away, but I remember Monica. If I've gone off the deep end, I've dragged her along with me, and I owe it to her to see this through and examine the source of my crazy.

Brad pulls the glass jar out of the fridge with the reverence of a high priest. The corporate queen gives him an epic frown of doubt and annoyance. I roll my eyes while he's not looking.

That's when I see them. Hanging like a pair of withered red prunes from a spindly limb, I see them. Gleanna nuts. Not as big or robust as the ones the elf had in his tree, but those had to be gleanna nuts. I take a deep breath and even though I'm standing a few feet back I can smell them--the rich magical scent, the Cinnamon Ultra Pumpkinator scent. Even without the taste in my mouth I feel like I could hover a few feet above the ground if I wanted to.

Corporate queen still looks doubtful, even when Brad wafts the scent towards her.

"What is this...dying plant thing? It seems--unimpressive," she says.

"It's like...a special breed of cinnamon. Developed in the far east by a hidden subculture of tree dwelling forest people. They're super in touch with nature and things."

I raise an eyebrow. Does Brad believe this, or is he lying to his queen? It's hard to tell, since he's looking at the withered little plant like it's the most precious thing he's ever seen. I swear, his eyes are watering and not because they're itchy and red from allergies.

"So how do you prepare this--new cinnamon?" Corporate queen asks.

"I just grate some into the Cinnamon Ultra Pumpkinators," he says. "Like some people do with nutmeg. I don't do it all the time. I've been trying to test it--just a little at a time, you know, to see how it goes over. But when I put it in, we sell out. When I don't, nothing. And you have to try it. The feeling it gives is...magical."

I gasp. Brad has totally been slipping his customers, including me, a magical mickey.

By the look on her face, this thought has also occurred to the corporate queen.

"You have been giving our customers an unauthorized ingredient with possible hallucinogenic and euphoric effects?" she asks. I don't know what she has planned for Brad, but she's projecting a chilly quiet certainty that makes me shiver.

"Nah, it's not like that," Brad protests. But corporate queen is already turning to leave, and she's punching messages into her phone with the speed and force of a woman possessed. She strides past me. I step out of her way and look back at Brad. If he chases her, he might leave the gleanna branch, and that would be my perfect opportunity to swipe it.

But he doesn't chase her or let go of the branch. "Wait," he screams. "You have to listen! It's amazing! It's *magic*!" His voice cracks on the last word, and the floor starts to shake as though we're having an earthquake. Corporate queen is thrown to the ground. Before I can think, I float off the ground, high enough that my fairy crown brushes the ceiling.

Brad is still yelling. "Magic!" he says. "It's fucking magic! We can all be magic! We have the *power*!"

Oh my god, I think, not if most people are going to handle it like you, Mr. Crazypants. For the first time, I'm totally sympathetic to the old elf not wanting to share his magic nuts.

Brad waves the wilted plant like a wand and the floor splits. From her position on the floor, corporate queen twists her mouth into a displeased grimace. He looms over her, still waving his sad little twig. Drain pipes snake out of the chasm like ropes and wrap around her ankles and wrists.

I'm frozen, or rather floating. What should I do? Should I try to wrestle with Brad and grab the twig? Would that put an end to his magical tirade or infuriate him and make it worse? I look around for a weapon or something, but CaffeineFreek's knives are better for slicing sandwiches than intimidating psychos 'roid-raging on magic. Even the giant industrial coffee makers are empty, so I can't dump hot water on him which might be a bad idea anyway since I don't want to accidentally splash the corporate queen. Think quicker, I tell myself, or he's going to kill her and maybe me and continue doping the town if I don't...

Luckily, like the best movie villains (or maybe the worst? I guess that depends on your point of view), Brad chooses this moment to start monologuing. He goes on and on, blah blah blah, no one understand me, why can't girls see what a nice guy I am, blah blah blah. He alternately looms over the corporate queen and threatens her with his twig then pleads with her to understand and forgive and maybe show him her titties?

She raises an eyebrow, as though this is the most annoying thing she's ever had to deal with and only fear of her imminent death is keeping her from rolling her eyes and telling him where to shove his stupid twig.

While Brad's moaning something about his childhood bullies, I finally spot it--the fire extinguisher. I swoop down to try to snatch it from its place about the sink, but I'm not that good at swooping and it's more firmly attached to the wall than I expected. I crash noisily against the faucet, and by the time I've disentangled my tutu, Brad is advancing.

"And I have to deal with crazy, annoying teenage girls like you ALL day! I mean, how hard is it to pass out coffee samples, Crystal!?" Brad yells. "And your little stunt in the tree nearly revealed my plans!"

"Yeah, well, you sweat too much, and your breath smells like moldy cheese!" I yell back.

He raises the wilted twig. I lift the nozzle on the fire extinguisher. He waves his sad little plant. I leap into the air to dodge his blow. The sink bursts, and my head smacks against the ceiling. I struggle to remember the instructions on how to work the fire extinguisher. Just as Brad aims at me again, I remember safety training day from chemistry lab.

I aim the nozzle at Brad's face and spray him with the white foam. He screeches and wipes at his eyes.

From behind him, the corporate queen slips out of her bonds. She rises to her feet, clutching one of her stiletto heels by the toe. She smashes the pointed heel into Brad's neck with all her might. He yelps and turns toward her, and I see my chance. His hands are slippery from the foam. I swoop towards him and grab for the twig.

The twig is slick, but my hands have a thin coating of glitter dust from my costume which gives me a little grip. I pull the twig out of Brad's hand and... the most peculiar feeling comes over me.

My head is rushing, and I feel invincible. I can do anything. Brad is waving his arms angrily but who cares? I wave the wand and he falls back. I give it a glorious upward sweep and the crack in the floor mends itself. I feel every subtle movement of the air around me like my skin is electrified, and I feel like I can hear the voice of the earth itself.

I'm about to see how high I can fly and if I can take the whole building with me when Monica walks in, still holding a cleaning rag. She raises an eyebrow, and I start to sink to the ground again.

"Too much?" I ask. My voice sounds as if it's coming from very far away.

"Way too much," she says.

The twig vibrates in my hand. It feels as though it's alien and mysterious, even frightening, and that it's been a part of me forever and I should never let it go. That letting it go is unbearable, unthinkable. Sickening. Monica looks at me, and I can tell she's hesitating to say something, which is weird because she's always been comfortable telling me what's on her mind, or at least she was. My head feels like its swirling and I'm on a roller coaster and I'm not sure, but I think maybe I want to get off. The ride has lasted long enough. Too long.

From far away I hear Brad moan. He's still on the floor--I must have thrown him harder than I thought. Corporate queen is peering over him, her face flickering between disgust, compassion, and a sharp analytical inquisitiveness. She must feel me looking at her, because she turns. Her glasses are broken.

"I'm sorry," I say. I feel my feet hit the floor for the first time in...it can't have been that long but it feels like forever, like time is moving too fast. Monica is by my side, and she puts her hand on my shoulder. It's warm and smells like the bleach solution CaffeineFreek employees use to clean tables. I stifle a giggle.

"I guess we're done now?" I ask. I'm not sure who I'm asking.

"Yes, I think that the store should temporarily close for repairs, and ummm, staff retraining. You will be notified when you can resume your duties," corporate queen answers. She has the stern, intense look of a woman anticipating a battle over whether the insurance company covers random acts of magic.

"Okay then," I say. The twig isn't pulsing or vibrating as much anymore, and I'm able to lower it. My arm is super tired, as though I've been lifting a huge weight and not some puny twig. "What should I..."

"Here," Monica says. At some point most of the mugs must have been smashed, but she's scrounged up a metal coffee shaker that's only a little dented. "I filled it with water. Put it in here."

I know she's talking about the twig and I hate myself a little for how much I'm hesitating. I take a deep breath and think about Brad and how crazy he got. Maybe I wouldn't get that crazy but maybe I would. Who can know for sure? Doesn't everyone have a dark side? I gulp and drop it into the shaker. Quick and sharp, so I don't have to think about it too much. I sway on my feet and think I might throw up but then I don't. It's okay.

Monica pats my hand. "That's good, Crystal. Let's go home."

"Nope, nope, hold on," I manage to get out before dashing towards the sink. I throw up everything I think I've ever eaten in my life, and it smells like sour milk and cinnamon.

Monica tells my mother I got food poisoning from some shrimp we had at her house. I spend three days in bed. If my mother suspects it's not food poisoning at all but something more like an "intense chemical dependency on caffeine and cinnamon," she's good enough not to say anything. Though she does book me three, yes, *three* appointments with Bev for next week. Monica brings my schoolwork.

Saints and Curses

There are lurid headlines all over social media about Brad, usually something about using CaffeineFreek for raves after hours or possible exploitation of young female workers. Everything described in breathless, pruriently outraged terms and all caps, of course. Reporters and wannabe reporters try to interview my mom and follow Monica to school.

I feel...I don't know. It's not like I really wanted the power to destroy the world or anything. But the magic was the most special, most...well, magical thing that's ever happened to me. I mean, I could *fly*. And it was the best thing I've ever felt before. And it was gone, maybe forever.

Monica told me. She took the twig to the tree in her yard, and somehow it melded into the trunk or something and now the elves are happy. The last magic in our world, probably, and I didn't get to see it.

Even a good Cinnamon Ultra Pumpkinator doesn't make me feel better. Don't get me wrong, without the magic they're still delicious and amazing, but I don't get that tingling excitement or the sense of endless possibilities. And CaffeineFreek takes them off the menu after a couple of weeks.

Monica comes by every day until I'm well enough to go back to school. I apply for the same colleges she does, but Monica's probably going to fancy-pants U while I head off to local community college. I don't want to think about being old and grown up now that I know for sure that magic is real.

I perk up once Spring rolls around. I get more college acceptances than I thought I would thanks to a powerful personal essay about my experiences with addiction and mental health issues. But that's not what really makes me feel better.

I first notice it on my way to Monica's the other day. Nibbles is draped over a branch off the tree, which has burst into bright golden leaves and vibrant flowers. No one has seen it so alive in years and looking at it makes me happy.

I reach up to pet Nibbles, who still hasn't forgiven me for the whole cinnamon-vomit incident but is looking rather peaceable at the moment. That's when I spot it. A small nut, barely more than a bud. Something like an acorn, but not. I touch it lightly with my fingers, and a thrill runs through me. I'm not an expert on acorns or nuts, but I know this one. A gleanna.

"Thank you," I say though I don't know who I'm talking to, since Nibbles certainly isn't listening and doesn't have anything to do with magic nuts on a tree anyway. I don't want to pick it or take it off the tree, at least not yet. It belongs here for a while longer. But looking at it reminds me that the magic is there, somewhere. And I can find it.

ERLKONIG

I never loved my son's mother. I met Marisol at a bar during the World Series--we were both drunkenly cheering for the same team. When our team won, there was excitement, more drinking, and then clumsy, exuberant sex. I might not have remembered her name after all these years, had she not showed up at my door two months later with a pregnancy test still wet with piss.

"I'll straighten out," Marisol promised, twirling a piece of frizzy black hair around her fingers. She did for a while. I held her hand at AA meetings and doctor's appointments, watching our son grow from a bud with flapping arms to a curled-up infant. I wasn't in the delivery room, though. She broke down the last month, wrecked her car, had a blood alcohol level through the roof. The docs gave her an emergency c-section, and there I was, a new dad, three hours late to my son's birth, ten hours too late to keep his mother from drinking herself off a cliff.

They gave me full custody. Marisol tried for a couple of supervised visits, her head hung down in shame the whole time.

Deep scratches ran down her arms and circled her neck. At the time, I worried they were track marks.

"He needs you," I said, "Pull it together." She hadn't washed her hair, and she stared ahead, her eyes the flat black of slick, wet roads. Before she left, she held him close and kissed his round little nose, which looked exactly like hers.

"Everyone close to me gets hurt," she said when she handed him back to me. She never came back.

Maybe because the kid had such a tough start in life, maybe because something changes inside a man when he holds his son for the first time, but I never felt so passionately protective of anyone until I had Ollie. He was a fighter. His muscles were weak after his traumatic birth, so docs said he might be late on crawling, walking, all that. But he kicked and squirmed and wiggled so hard, I swear he was working out, building strength, just goddamned *determined*. Met every milestone, even talking early. And once he started talking, he didn't stop until he collapsed into bed at night, worn out. Until the sickness, anyway.

Looking back, I'm sure he was sick longer than I'd thought-- he just had so much energy, like a young pup.

There was an endless cycle of doctors and diagnosis, vitamins and medicines and treatment plans. Leukemia, they finally said, a rare kind. Radiation and chemo and remission. We had good years. He played baseball, climbed trees, built snow forts. But the cancer came back, or something did, something that sucked the life out of him.

He'd get dreams, you see, right before the cancer would come back. Wake up screaming. Scratches on his throat. I thought he might have done it himself, while he was sleeping. But he shook his head and clung to my arm.

90

"He's...it's coming for me," he said. "He's huge and dark and has long thin fingers that grab me."

"It's okay, kiddo. I'm here. I won't go away until you're asleep," I told him. He shivered in bed, tangled up in blankets, eyes wide open until dawn.

I asked his most recent doc about the dreams. He gave me a lecture on night terrors, sleep paralysis, lots of big words--but no solutions. Sleeping drugs were too strong for his age or interfered with his other medications.

I finally took poor Ollie to my Nonna, who was positively ancient and had raised enough kids to fill a hospital ward five times over. Her eyes watered when she saw Ollie, and she took his thin, white chin in her gnarled fingers, turning his head this way and that.

"Malocchio," she murmured. "Evil eye. Check room for cold air and hang corno charm over bed." She searched through one of those enormous old jewelry boxes that old women have that seem to leak necklace chains and mismatched beads. She pulled out a necklace with a carved goat horn charm and handed it to me.

You might wonder why I bought into all this "evil eye" stuff, since I was a sensible guy who didn't go in for magical mumbo jumbo. The only thing I can say is that I knew better than to discount anything Nonna said. So, I went home and hung the "corno" necklace over Ollie's bed. He stopped having the dreams.

Leukemia kept gnawing at him, though. Sometimes he seemed like he was winning the fight, other times...it didn't. Fevers, chills, nausea from the chemo. Night sweats that left his sheets soaking wet. And those damned scratches. I don't know where he got those scratches all the time--red welts circling his neck, running down his arms. At one point I lost it at a night nurse.

"What the fuck are you doing to him? Where are all these scratches coming from?" I yelled.

She looked at me oddly. "I don't see any scratches, sir. Could you show me what you're talking about?"

"Look, you blind ... look right here on his arm--it's bleeding and swollen and..."

She stared at where I was pointing. Ollie looked up at her hopefully. Then she slowly backed away and mumbled something about getting the doctor. She came back with a headshrinker. I must have turned purple trying to keep from screaming.

The shrink was one of those fresh-faced earnest types that emerge from Unis all gung-ho to save people. She asked me some questions about grief and Ollie's prognosis, then handed me a fistful of pills and prescription for more.

"Let me know if you see the scratches again," she said, giving me a tremulous smile and wiping her eyes. "These kinds of hallucinations happen when caregivers have the stress of watching a loved one decline."

I resisted the urge to spit the pills back in her face—that would earn me a trip to the psych ward for sure, and I needed to take care of Ollie. So, I swallowed the pills and promised I'd get the scripts filled. I checked Ollie out of that hospital soon as I could.

At home, things got worse. He rolled around in bed, half-awake, hot to the touch, mumbling. Scratches bloomed across his chest, growing outward like the red branches of a burning tree. Sometimes Ollie lashed out at me, as though he didn't recognize who I was. I didn't know what to do--Nonna had passed on a while back. I called a priest, but the one who came was a milk-faced sop with trembling hands. His eyes lingered too long on the bare skin that peaked out of Ollie's nightshirt, so I got rid of him.

That night, Ollie started talking to people and things only he could see. He hid under his blankets every time tree branches scratched against his window.

"He's trying to get in here," he told me. "He wants to take me with him, under the ground..."

"You're not going anywhere, kiddo," I tried to reassure him. Just in case, I looked out the window—nothing but cold black tree limbs and swirling snow.

"He's right out there...he's...ooh..." Ollie clutched his belly. I helped him to the bathroom, but he didn't throw up. Instead, bright red blood bloomed on the bottom of his boxer shorts. He put his head down on the toilet seat, and tears leaked out of his eyes.

I started to sweat. "We've got to get to an emergency room, Ollie." I called 9-1-1. Nothing but static and an eerie shriek that made me jump. I dropped the phone, and it went dead.

I cursed under my breath. "No ambulance, then. I'll drive you."

"No! Don't take me out there...it's waiting..." his voice weakened and trailed away. His boxers were soaked, red and black. I pulled them off and wiped the blood off his legs. I thought about putting him in a depends to absorb the blood, but he was already agitated, and he hated wearing them. Better to put down some towels on the seat of the car.

I wrapped him in every blanket in the house, but he still shivered like mad when I carried him into the garage. I strapped him in the back seat and cranked up the heater. When I opened the garage door, I saw the swirls of snow I'd seen out Ollie's window had grown into thick white drifts that sparkled in my headlights. Icy flurries fell so heavily on the roof of my car I could hear muffled taps as each one landed. An ice-laden tree branch cracked against my windshield and scraped over the car roof as I pulled out of the driveway.

"It's trying to get in the car..." Ollie murmured.

"Shhh, it's okay, kiddo, it's just a tree branch," I said. But the hair on the back of my neck rose, and I turned around to peer back into the darkness. The tree loomed out of the night, long thin fingers reaching towards the car, grasping and scratching...no. The wind was blowing it, that was all.

I drove as fast as I dared on treacherous roads. Blizzard must've knock out the power, because even the stoplights looked like cold, dead metallic arms. I found myself longing for a red light, sign of life along the empty road. The wind howled.

"Do you hear it?" Ollie asked. "He's calling me..."

I shivered. "Just the wind," I said, as much to myself as him. Unearthly moaning filled the car, and I longed to press my hands against my ears to shut out the sound. I punched the button on the radio. Nothing came on but that goddamned static and an emergency signal that grew into a maddening shriek. I shut it off, took a deep breath, and tried to focus on the road. It was hard to see through the thickly falling snow.

"Up ahead!" Ollie screamed. "Look there! He's sent them after me! White witches!"

I blinked and shook my head. "No, no, it can't be. They're snowmen in someone's yard." Why the fuck would someone build those creepy things, I wondered. Looming shapes studded with shards of ice, their faces twisted in grotesque snarls. They seemed to move, but that had to be an illusion, the motion of the car or the falling snow distorting reality.

Maybe I shouldn't have thrown away that shrink's prescriptions.

Now Ollie's struggling in his seat, slapping his hands wildly, screaming and clawing like a hellcat. "He's got me! He's taking me!"

I didn't say anything this time, just hit the gas. Fuck the weather, Fuck the ice. I slid and spun and burned rubber all the way to the hospital. Drove straight to the emergency room doors, right up on the sidewalk. I smashed the horn to call for help, then struggled out of the car into a cold, wet snow drift. Nearly pulled the handle off the back door trying to get it open.

Ollie had gone silent. He was pale and cold. I huddled him in my arms, the way I had when he was a baby, pressed close to me so I could keep him warm. I didn't want to know.

I kicked open the hospital doors. Night nurses and a bleary-eyed doc took him out of my arms. They laid him out on gurney. Shouting, CPR, needles and IV's. I stood there, chilled to the bone. Blood trickled out his mouth. The doc wiped his brow and crossed himself. So sorry, they said. Cancer, it's too bad, he was so young, poor kid. Are you alright, sir?

Not alright. Never again. I held Ollie's hand. His eyes were wide open, terrified. I closed them, kissed his forehead one last time. Then I slipped out of the hospital into the darkness. It was waiting outside, howling, moaning. I took off my jacket, sweater, everything. I watched the scratches bloom on my arms, from ice as sharp as broken glass. I felt its breath on my face, a cold so intense it could crack your bones. I closed my eyes. I wouldn't have to wait long.

Lantgen

THE LOST CAT

I get off work late. Clay took the car to go out with his buddies, so I walk home. I hear a piercing meow coming from the dumpster outside my favorite Italian place. I keep walking, thinking some tomcats must be fighting, but the sound grows louder and more desperate.

There must be a cat trapped in the dumpster. I lift the heavy metal lid, and sure enough, there's a cat in there, yowling and hissing and fluffed up.

"It's okay, kitty-kitty, you can come out now," I say. But the cat doesn't move. It's a big tom, mostly white with some black markings on its back. I look down to see if it's injured. It seems healthy, but it's tangled in something. I work with injured animals at the pound, so I know how animals act when they're cornered and upset. I start talking to the kitty, nice and low, then I lean in close enough to wrap my coat around him so he can't scratch me.

He hisses something awful as I lift him out of the dumpster, but once he's outside the bin he freezes. Poor thing. He must be too scared to fight anymore. I take my coat off him, but he's still tangled up with a string of garlic. He must have been looking for something to eat in the dumpster when someone threw out the restaurant leftovers.

I untangle the strands of garlic from around the poor kitty. I expect him to flee at once, but he doesn't. Instead, he sits on the sidewalk, looking up at me. What a strange cat! He isn't fearful, at least not once I get the garlic off him. And even in the dim light covered in bits of old spaghetti, he's beautiful.

His fur is thick and soft and pure white where it's clean, with one deep black patch on his back like a cute little cape. And he sits beside the dumpster with his paws neatly tucked in and lifts his head like a dapper little gentleman. His eyes--striking! I've never seen a cat with eyes that shade of deep burgundy red. If it hadn't been for the black in his fur, I might have thought he was an albino.

I sigh as I look at him. If it wasn't for Clay, I'd take him home with me. He isn't any ordinary street cat, and it would be so nice to have a soft, sweet cat to cuddle with. But I remember my poor, sweet Mittens and what Clay did to her, so I don't. I just sigh and give him a pat. He purrs and licks tomato sauce off his paws. Then I steel myself and turn away to go home.

I don't realize at first that he's following me. He moves silently, and I might not have noticed him at all, except I look back and catch a gleam of red eyes looking out of a dark corner. Poor kitty. He must be lonely and want a friend. I know how it feels. I'll leave some food in the alleyway near our apartment when I get back.

The streetlight outside our building flickers and burns out as I make my way up the front steps. There isn't anyone around, not even the usual bums sleeping on the sidewalk. The foyer smells like greasy takeout, and the stairs are sticky with--well,

I'm not sure I want to know. I've found used condoms, empty liquor bottles, and cigarette butts all over the stairwells. When I get to my hallway it's eerie quiet, as though I'm the only living person in the whole place. My steps echo down the silent hall, the only sound apart from the wail of a distant siren.

I let myself into the apartment and shut the door behind me, fast. It's too late and I'm too tired to want to watch TV, but I flip it on anyway, so I don't feel too alone. I'm settling in bed when I hear a noise outside the window. I wonder if it's the TV, which I leave on while I'm falling asleep. No--it's coming from outside on the fire escape. I'm wide awake, blood thudding in my veins.

I don't think a criminal would climb up this high to break into the apartment. It's six stories up!

I've almost convinced myself it's nothing when I hear it again--a soft pat-pat. My stomach clenches. What should I do? Call the cops?

Don't be stupid. The cops already think you're a hysterical bitch. That's what Clay told them, and that one cop laughed. If I call them now and it's nothing maybe they won't come the next time, even if his hands are squeezing my throat and I've got black spots in my eyes and...

Stop and breathe. Overreacting. That's what I'm doing. I do it all the time, he says.

Just go and check what's out the window. It's probably nothing--just some clothes or something hanging outside. But I can't seem to make myself move.

There's another pattering sound, then a delicate "meowrr?" The trilling sound a cat makes. Relief surges through me.

I get up and look out the window. Sure enough, there's a cat out there, sitting on the ledge and batting the glass with his paw.

Not just any cat, my cat, the poor dumpster cat with spaghetti sauce on his paws. I open the window.

"What are you doing up here, kitty-kitty?" I ask. "It's too high up and you'll hurt yourself if you fall."

The cat purrs and rubs his head on my hand, begging me to take him in. And I want to. I'm so lonely in this empty apartment and I miss having a cat curled up on my feet or against my back in bed.

"I want to, kitty," I say, though yes, I know how stupid and crazy it sounds talking out loud to a cat. "I want to let you in, but...he'll hurt you."

Mittens had been hiding under the sofa. He jerked her out and opened the window. I saw what he planned to do. I screamed and tried rip Mittens away from him. He shoved me, hard. I fell back and smashed my head against the coffee table. Mittens hissed and scratched, and he'd reached his arm back...

This other cat looks at me with those gorgeous red eyes, and I think, it wouldn't be so bad to let him in for a minute, give him some food to eat. Clay probably won't be back for hours, maybe not at all tonight, if he starts serious drinking. I could let the cat out in the morning and Clay'd never even know. I could try to find a shelter or something to take the poor kitty in.

The kitty purrs and trills. His fur is bunny-soft beneath my fingers and petting him make me feel so...comforted.

"Alright," I say. "You can come in."

As though he's been waiting for me to say something like that, he streaks into the house like a bolt of fuzzy lightening.

"Would you like some food, kitty?" I ask. I don't have any cat food left--I donated it to a shelter when Mittens...disappeared. I'd searched the alleyway, calling for her. I'd sobbed and looked for her broken body. I remember rough concrete on my hands and digging through garbage cans and finding a dozen alley cats but no sign of Mittens. I'd woken up, cold and aching, where I'd fallen asleep on the sidewalk.

I don't have any food for him, but the new kitty just curls up at the foot of my bed and looks like he'd rather sleep than eat. I don't mind.

Sleepiness floods through me again. I feel safer with the cat here, which is stupid because who ever heard of a cat protecting anyone from anything, apart from loneliness? But my eyelids are heavy, and I sink back down in bed.

My last thought before I fall asleep--Henry. It's the cat's name, and I know it as surely as I know my own. Soft weight settles near the back of my neck, then oblivion.

I wake in the morning to the smell of stale beer. Clay must have stumbled home sometime in the night. He's drawn the shades tight and closed the window. Normally, he wakes me up, but I guess I slept more soundly than usual. He's sleeping soundly too, his face pale and moist as a fish's underbelly. He must not have even noticed Henry, who's still curled up at the foot of the bed.

After he'd hurt Mittens, I'd wondered what to do. I could've stayed on the sidewalk, homeless. I could've gone back to my mother's. She'd likely have had her thighs wrapped around a new man, someone who'd eye me appraisingly. She would have told me everything was my fault for being a whore.

I went back. Clay was there, waiting for me. He said he was sorry, cried a little bit. He wanted me to feel sorry for him, like he was some poor dupe who couldn't help murdering my cat. My sweet baby Mittens. He said he'd buy me a new one, a better one, as though cats are like broken glasses or smashed plates and don't have feelings.

"Come on kitty," I whisper to Henry. "He can't find you here." My first thought is to shoo him back out the fire escape. But it's so high up, I get vertigo even thinking about letting him out there. Anyway, Henry seems impossible to wake. He's limp and heavy as a stack of wet towels. Until I bring him near the window.

The second sunlight streaks across him he yowls like his tail's on fire. I hurry him away from the light, afraid he'll wake Clay. Maybe those red eyes are a sign he has an allergy or sensitivity to sunlight. I think I read that somewhere.

I can't leave him for Clay to find, and there's only one place in the apartment that's dark and Clay won't go--the laundry room. It's not really our laundry room, but no one else on our floor uses it, so I figure it's safe. I put Henry in a basket with some dirty clothes, which he doesn't seem to mind, and lug him over to the laundry. I leave some tuna in a dish and hope that no one notices the poor kitty before I get back from work. Luckily, Henry doesn't seem inclined to meow or draw attention to himself. That cat must sleep like the dead.

When I get home, Clay's surly and foul, but he doesn't say much. I wonder if he's getting sick--he seems listless and tired, as if some of his usual rage got drained out of him. He grumbles about food, and I make some chicken. It's his favorite, which mellows him out a little.

"I'm just going to run a load of laundry real fast," I say. I managed to sneak some food into a basket, hiding it beneath a load of Clay's work clothes.

When I get to the laundry room, Henry is wide awake. He purrs when he sees me. The can of tuna I left is untouched, but a large rat lies stiff and slumped against the washer.

"Aren't you a clever boy!" I say. The rat doesn't look eaten, though it's neck is snapped and there's a smear of blood on Henry's muzzle, which he cleans with his paw. I throw in a load of laundry and chuck out the old tuna. I wonder if I can sneak Henry back in the apartment tonight, or if I should just try to take him outside. Neither seems like a good option. Clay will notice if I'm gone too long, and I can't bear to let him see Henry. I know him--he might seem okay at first, even welcoming. Then he'd use Henry to hurt me. In the end I just leave the laundry room door open and hope Henry can find a safe way out.

Back in the apartment, Clay stares sullenly at the TV while I fold laundry. I want to believe that everything will be alright, but there's a tension rising in the room, like an invisible line being pulled tight. I fumble with the laundry, and Clay's lip curls. His team must be losing, because he's glaring at the screen.

There's a noise at the door. I freeze. I know that sound--Henry. He's meowing and patting the door. Clay looks up, and I know he can hear it too.

"What's that?" he asks. "Sounds like a cat."

"I'm sure it's nothing." I scramble to the door, but I'm so stupid and clumsy, I trip over the laundry basket. Clay gives me a suspicious look and gets up to open the door. Before I can do anything, Henry streaks into the room. He nudges my leg with his muzzle, and gives a plaintive meow, as though he's afraid I'm hurt. Or he's hungry. It can be hard to tell with cats.

Clay's standing over me, his eyebrows raised. "Is that cat yours?"

"I just found him trapped somewhere and got him loose. He followed me home, Clay, I swear, I didn't bring him here..."

Clay's face is unreadable. He scrutinizes Henry, who tucks his furry face into the crook of my arm. It's such a sweet cat gesture I can't help but pet him, and something about Henry's warm snuggles gives me a resolve I haven't felt in a long time. If Clay hurts Henry, I tell myself, I'll leave. I'll leave for good this time, no matter what. Henry purrs.

Clay steps back. "I don't know about that cat. There's something about him. Those eyes are uncanny. Devil eyes, if you ask me."

"He's just a cat like any other. I think he might be an albino."

"He'd better not cause any trouble."

"He won't, I'll make sure of it, you'll barely notice he's here..."

Clay grunts. There's the sound of cheering on the TV, and he goes to check the score. I keep folding my laundry, with Henry curled up beside me.

That night Henry sleeps with his back pressed against me, between me and Clay. I pet him as I drift off. My eyes slowly close. Safe.

I stir in the night, my consciousness emerging from dreamy, watery depths. Moonlight streams through the bedroom curtains. There's a rumbling growl, then an angry hiss. I see a flash of sharp teeth. Clay moans in his sleep, then there's a horrible noise, licking and sucking and low growling. I want to wake up, but my limbs are so heavy and dull with sleep I can't move. After a while, the noises fade into the background like a bad dream and I sink back into oblivion.

The next morning, the light feels harsh and over bright. Henry's retreated under the bed, away from the sunlight that bothers him so much. Clay stirs fitfully.

"What time is it?" he asks.

"Eight thirty."

"Christ, I'm late," he mutters. He throws his legs off the edge of the bed and tries to sit up. He grabs his head with both hands. "What the fuck did I drink last night?"

"The usual," I say. "Are you feeling sick?"

"Yeah." He lays back down. "Woozy."

"I'll get you some gatorade, and there might be some of that herbal hangover cure leftover in the bathroom." I get up to check. The cure is long gone, so I bring a couple of aspirin and a big glass of water instead. When I get back, Clay is rubbing his neck. His skin has a clammy, unhealthy pallor and his eyes are red-rimmed.

"Maybe you should call in sick to work today," I say.

"Don't be a moron. I missed last week because that shitty car of yours got a flat, and now that fucker Jameson has me on notice." Clay takes the aspirin and downs the water. "Bring me something to eat."

I pour a bowl of cereal and add some milk. I'll need to go shopping today to get some cat food and a litterbox. Now that I think about it, it's strange that Henry hasn't eaten anything, or even used the bathroom as far as I can tell.

I take the cereal to Clay, who eats like he hasn't seen food in days. I refill the bowl three times before he's satisfied. I guess I should buy cereal too.

That day at work I keep thinking about the strange dream I had the night before. It gives me the shivers. Is there something wrong with Henry?

I buy some cat food on my lunch break, the canned beef flavor, since Henry doesn't eat tuna.

I get home after dark, and Henry rubs against my legs as I come in the door. I open a can of food, but he won't eat it, though he seems hungry. I got some burgers for me and Clay, and I offer Henry a bit of ground beef, but he won't eat that either. Instead, he knocks the bloody butcher paper the meat in off the counter and licks it clean. Weird, but he had been living on the streets. Maybe he's used to eating trash.

Clay comes home in a foul mood. He's got dark circles under red-rimmed eyes, and he gives me a glare that makes me shrivel up inside. But he's in no condition to fight, and Clay only picks fights he can win. He flops in front of the TV and looks like he has to strain to lift the burger I make for him.

I let out the breath I'm holding. He falls asleep on the couch, his burger half eaten in front of him. I clear it away.

The sounds of the city seem far away. A light breeze stirs the curtains, and Henry bats at them as they dance lightly on the windowsill. The moonlight stains his white coat silver-grey, like a living shadow. He has the grace of a predator.

I flip channel to a show I like and cover Clay with an extra blanket. One time, not long after he hurt Mittens, he came down with a severe case of flu. I took off work to care for him, and I felt guilty for thinking how nice it was to have him weak and helpless in bed. I didn't look over my shoulder or walk on eggshells. I didn't measure every word with the care and precision of an artist fitting together pieces of stained glass. Even caring for him--bringing him soup and medicine, holding the bucket while he retched--gave me a perverse pleasure. Every act of servitude reminded me of how weak he was, and how for the first time, I was in control. Then he got better.

I go to bed. For the first time, Henry doesn't curl up in bed with me. He sits on the windowsill, his red eyes bright, cleaning his paws.

In the morning, Clay can hardly stand up, much less get off the couch. I offer to call a doctor, even though I know he'll refuse, which he does with a curt gesture. I bring him some cereal and help him eat. His mouth contorts with frustration and rage.

"Something bit me last night," he mutters. "It's probably from sleeping on this stupid couch. Why didn't you wake me up so I could get in bed?"

Because only the stupid and the brave wake a sleeping bear, I want to answer. I may not be brave, but maybe I'm not as stupid as he thinks. I press my lips together to keep words like these from tumbling out of my mouth. Instead, I shrug.

"It was probably a rat or something big," he continues. "Guess the fucking cat you got is useless when it comes to rats. Figures."

"Should I call the super for an exterminator?"

"Don't be stupid, we're in an illegal sublet. The super doesn't give a fuck about rats anyway. Get the peroxide and clean out the bite."

"Okay." I find the peroxide and cotton balls in bathroom cupboard. When I get back Clay peevishly pulls back the collar of his shirt.

There are two small puncture wounds on his neck, close together. They look swollen and red, and I wonder if they're getting infected. Clay hollers and flails at me when I douse them in peroxide, pain giving him surprising strength. I'll probably have a couple of bruises.

"I'm just trying to help," I say. My face is a mask of kindness. I'm the good nurse. The loving wife.

Clay's eyes narrow. Good liars always smell a lie. But he doesn't say anything more, and I start getting ready to go to work.

As I'm leaving, he asks, "Where's the cat?"

I keep my good wife mask firmly in place. "I let him out early this morning." Then I close the door behind me. Henry is no doubt asleep in his place under the bed, but Clay's too tired and too sick to search for him. And if he finds him, I think he'll regret it.

I don't come home until after dark. Since Henry liked meat wrappings, I bought some more ground beef. This time I'll make a meatloaf.

The apartment is silent when I come in. I check on Clay. His breath is shallow, and his skin has the damp paleness of drowned things. The wounds on his neck have grown, and they ooze thin trickles of blood.

I hear the scrape of claws in the kitchen, and I freeze. It's only Henry. He lets out a happy meow and bounds over to me, soft head butting my leg. I reach down to pet him.

"Who's a good kitty-kitty," I say, and he purrs. The litterbox is still empty, and he hasn't touched the cat food I left. Then again, I didn't expect him to.

I mix the ingredients for the meatloaf together then shape it and stick it in the oven. I put the meat wrapper on the floor for Henry, who licks it greedily. I bought a little cat toy, a stuffed mouse that dangles from a string. I get him to chase it all over the apartment while I wait for the meatloaf to cook.

I check on Clay again. His eyes flicker dully. I suppose I could call a doctor without waking him up. That might be for the best--if something does happen, there'd be less suspicion.

Suspicion? What am I thinking? I quake with silent laughter. Who would believe even half of the truth? Everyone would think Clay was a crazy if he tried to tell them what was happening. I sometimes think I'm crazy just for thinking it, believing it.

Clay stirs fretfully then wakes. He stares at me. He knows. His mouth works. I lean in close to hear what he has to say.

"Wwwitch. And your ffffucking cat. No one will ever love you like I do."

I stroke his hair back with something like tenderness. He's too weak to push me away, though his spindly hands claw at my shirt.

"I'd rather die alone than live another day with you," I whisper to him, sweetly.

Henry hops on the couch, purring loudly. I rub his ears and he closes his eyes. Such soft fur.

Clay lasts through the night. I hear his rasping breath coming from the couch, though he doesn't speak to me again. I consider bringing him some water or a little food, but it seems cruel to prolong the inevitable. Henry snuggles next to me when I go to sleep, warm and peaceful. I ignore the dreams. In the morning he's resumed his spot under the bed. I hear a horrid rattling gasp.

I would not have thought a person could grow so gaunt so quickly. Clay is hard to recognize, more like a macabre wax figure than a human being. I call an ambulance and try to sound panicked. They arrive as Clay's last breath wheezes and creaks out of his swollen throat. An infection, the EMTs tell me, but when they think I can't hear them they whisper about overdoses and drugs, look at the injection tracks on his neck.

There's a whirlwind of activity--funeral planning, visits from friends I haven't seen in months, maybe years, painful phone calls to notify Clay's family and close friends. His mother has a breathy, nervous voice and she assures me that God has a plan. Maybe he does, I think. But sometimes people have other plans, too.

Clay's friends give me hearty hugs and condolences. Most of them are youngish men who look older than they should. They have whiskey breath and stubbly chins that scratch against my neck as they lean on my shoulders.

My mother visits, her eyes red and seeping. She stations herself in the center of the mourners.

"I loved him like my own son," she says, though she'd cursed me for marrying him. "Ran off with the first one to smile nice at you," she'd said then. "You are one dumb slut."

Those words ring in my ears as she gives me a stiff-armed hug after the funeral. When she finally leaves me in peace, I wonder how much money she thinks I'm getting from life insurance.

I go back to the apartment, the one I shared with Clay. It's packed up now. I found a new place in a nicer neighborhood. Henry is hidden under the bed, curled up in a dark corner the light never touches, sleeping.

He's been friendly and engaging with the people who visit in the evenings.

"I'm glad you finally got a new cat," someone said to me. "And he's so beautiful!"

He hasn't eaten anything I've tried to feed him, and I wonder how long I have before he gets hungry. I've read that lions who make a particularly large kill might go for several days without eating. It's been nearly a week.

Night falls, and Henry comes out from beneath the bed. I pet him. He purrs then gives my hand a playful bite. His teeth are sharp.

BRAIDS

For hundreds of years, the women of Mont Noire have been renowned for their hair. No matter what the color, their hair was thick and shining with a luster that made them the envy of all the surrounding villages. Even today, when Mont Noire women cut their hair in short, modern styles, the vibrancy of the colors and the luminous shine turns heads wherever they go. But in the past, when women wore their hair long, nothing could compare. They grew rivers of hair so black and shining it was like the heavens on a clear night, or glowing gold like a sunset, or like the earthen fire of a forge. Even age would not mar its beauty. The rich glow of polished chestnuts would become the silver of a moonlit stream or the crystalline white of the first snowfall.

The men of Mont Noire were not so blessed.

It was not always thus for the women either. Chroniclers noted that their hair was much like other womens', until the arrival of the Haar-witch.

No one knows exactly when Cresputina arrived in the village, and where she came from became a subject of many heated debates. Some insisted she came from the court of the great Emperor in the East, and that she'd fled to Mont Noire to escape poisonous political intrigues she'd stumbled into there. The advocates of this theory noted that she brought with her a wide variety of fine spices and scented oils that could only have come from the glorious cities of the Ancient Empire. Others suggested that she escaped from Espana, that she was a refugee from the Moorish wars or the terrible plague that had ravaged the southern countries, working its way slowly and inexorably north.

Whatever her history, Cresputina arrived in Mont Noire with little property besides a fine set of silver-plated combs, a mirror decorated with the sun and stars, and her collection of mysterious flasks and bottles that contained oils, powders, and scented herbs, many of which no one in Mont Noire had ever seen before.

She had little money and ragged clothes, and her thick accent and foreign ways made the local priest suspicious. Perhaps for that reason, no man would allow her to stay under his roof or even under the roof of his barn. But one of the village women took pity on her (the Bruliard family claim it was their ancient grandmere, but this is disputed by the Montagnes, who insist it was their wise auntie). Thus it was that Cresputina found her way to Mistress Birgitte, the kindly widow who ran the local alehouse.

Truth be told, Mistress Birgitte did not need an assistant. She had five daughters, and while two had married and left home, three remained to help her with the business, and they were good, hard-working girls. Yet, Cresputina's desperate plight moved the widow to take her in. Birgitte had her daughters fix a pallet by the hearth for her guest and promised to allow the strange woman to stay and work as long as she wished.

Cresputina's eyes flooded with tears at the widow's generosity. She pressed a hand to her heart and mumbled a choked up "merci, madame," before she tumbled onto the pallet and fell fast asleep. The next morning, Birgitte's eldest daughter came to wake her for breakfast but found Cresputina already bustling about the hearth.

Now this eldest girl was a sweet-faced lass with strong, capable hands, skilled at baking bread and tending her mother's garden. But alas, she had a lame foot and could only walk with the aid of a sturdy branch. For this reason, her beloved's family forbade their marriage, though he returned her love and would have no other wife. Cresputina learned all this from Birgitte, who chatted merrily as she tasted the latest batch of ale and kneaded the day's bread. The Haar-witch examined the unfortunate girl from the corner of her eye as she swept the hearth.

The lass set about her morning chores, kindling a fire, filling the kettle with fresh water for their breakfast pottage, and wiping down the tables. She had her hair wrapped in a kerchief, but when she sat down to eat, she pulled it back to wipe away sweat. Cresputina cringed when she saw the girl's hair. It was thin and brittle, the tips burnt from cooking over the fire. Brittle hair and broken bones, she thought, but I can help her.

Cresputina waited until the next feast-day, when the stars were right for healing. That evening, as the family put on their finery to attend Vespers and evening mass, she pulled the eldest girl aside. She sat her down and brushed out the girl's hair with her silver combs and smoothed it with scented oils. Then she twisted the strands into fine-woven braids. As she braided, she sang.

"Sturdy and strong, supple and long, straighten her limbs by the end of my song." The girl's hair grew thick and shining as it absorbed the spell from her fingers and the healing oil.

Birgitte's daughter relaxed under Cresputina's ministrations, until she drifted off to sleep. "Don't wake her," Cresputina said to Birgitte. "The poor thing exhausted herself so. We can return for her after the first service."

So it was that Birgitte's daughter woke to an empty house. "Oh, no," she thought, "I'll miss the service, and Father Bernard will be so angry!" And she ran out of the house, not even noticing that she'd forgotten the sturdy branch she carried to help her walk.

Her beloved was coming to church late as well. He walked along, whistling a tune he'd heard one of the older women singing, enjoying the quiet golden hour before he had to listen to the priest's angry sermons. Birgitte's daughter ran past him, and he stared at her. He could have sworn he'd never seen a girl so beautiful before, yet she had the face of his beloved. But she ran on two strong legs, and her hair was glossy and elegant, styled in a becoming way he'd never seen. He called after her, and when Birgitte's daughter heard his voice, she stopped and turned.

"How is it that you can run so fast?" he asked, bewildered. "Did you step out of my dreams?"

Her mouth fell open. She'd been running and it felt so good, so right, that she hadn't even thought...

"It's a miracle!" she exclaimed. "Unless...oh, all of a sudden, I'm frightened it won't last, and I'll be lame again tomorrow!" She lifted her skirt a bit and looked at him pleadingly. "Could you please check my limbs--very thoroughly, mind you--check them up and down to make sure they're as straight and supple as they should be?"

Her beloved's face flushed. "Quite gladly, my lady."

And only after he'd examined her body quite thoroughly to the satisfaction of them both, did they return to the church, where he knelt before the entire village and declared his love. With no objections from his family, they were married the next Sunday.

The young bride's happy fate and the miracle of her cure did not go unnoticed. Publically, the villagers proclaimed it was the work of God, or perhaps the Virgin Mary, or maybe one of the many saints. Privately, many came to visit Cresputina. Her lovely braids and other hairstyles became popular with women and girls throughout the village. She also did a brisk trade in headache cures and hair tonics for men, which were simple matters that rarely required real magic. Then there were the others.

One day a young woman came to the alehouse to speak to Cresputina. She had hair the color of polished walnut and a delicately pointed chin, and she introduced herself as Leda, the butcher's wife.

"I have been married for many a year," she said. "But I have not got with child even once. If I do not give my husband an heir soon, he will throw me out."

Cresputina raised her eyebrows. The butcher was a thick-fingered man with a round belly and a snow-white beard, well over sixty years old if he'd lived a day. His bride looked closer to twenty, with the bloom of health and youth on her face.

"How often does he...perform his husbandly duties?"

"He works at his shop every day besides the Sabbath," said Leda, without the tell-tale blush Cresputina expected.

"No, no, that's not what I mean. When was the last time he...came to your bed?"

"Well, we only have one bed, so that's where both he and I sleep."

Cresputina frowned. "Has he done naught but sleep in your marital bed?"

"What else is there to do?" the girl asked.

"Well, then he can hardly expect you to bear a child--"

Leda shook her head. "A woman is barren, not a man. Or so my husband says. If I do not have a child somehow, he will blame me and cast me out. And without his support, my mother and sisters will starve."

Cresputina tapped her lips with one finger, thinking. "I have just the thing for you," she said. She sat Leda down and combed out the girl's dark hair. Then she began to weave a simple spell. A braided crown for boldness and luck. A cascade of hair scented with spring flowers to evoke desire and ample curls to hold it fast.

"Go now," she said when she'd finished, "and find your man." When questioned later, Cresputina insisted she meant the girl's husband, and that she only intended to make Leda beautiful enough to raise the elderly butcher's flagging desire. But that is not how spells work. Magic loves a shortcut.

Leda, however, was not in the mood for a shortcut on her way home that evening. The breeze was cool and gentle, and just enough golden light remained when she left the alehouse that she decided to walk past a meadow where the berries had only just begun to ripen. She plucked a sweet red fruit and popped it in her mouth, and she could not remember eating anything quite so luscious before then.

She heard a soft sound near her, like a sigh, and she pulled back the brambles to see who was there. It was Gwaine, her husband's apprentice. He was near to her age, handsome but

116

shy. Why, he'd never looked her in the eye before! But now he bowed to her politely, and in the sunset he looked as gracious as a young knight.

Perhaps it was the heady scent of flowers in her hair, or the bright taste of the berry in her mouth, but bold thoughts arose in Leda's mind. She took Gwaine's hand, a smile on her lips. He knelt before her and spoke words that he'd never dared say aloud even in his dreams. But before he could finish speaking, her lips found his.

When Cresputina saw her a few months later, Leda was round and glowing. Her husband stood by her side, bragging of his prowess in his old age to anyone who would listen. His faithful apprentice followed behind them, careful to assist his master's wife in her delicate condition, a soft smile on his face.

Not long after Leda gave birth to a healthy, apple-cheeked little boy, Cresputina noticed another child. This one was small and dark-haired, and peeked at her from the local farrier's shop. The child's face was so dirty and its clothes so rough and shapeless that Cresputina could not tell whether it was male or female until her friend Birgitte told her. The little one was a girl, the alewife said, and the farrier was her uncle. Though he had no business caring for such a young girl, especially since he had no wife, he'd insisted on taking the girl as his apprentice instead of sending her to the convent school.

"He's a cruel master," the good widow said when the subject came up. Indeed, the farrier was a thin, miserly man with a patchy white beard that didn't quite hide his weasly chin. But his bony hands kept a firm grip on the long leather whip he used on spirited horses, and perhaps his spirited niece as well.

But the child, called Soot because of her dirty clothes, worked for her uncle without complaint until a few months after

Leda's baby was born. On that fateful day, the Lord of Dark Mountain flew into a rage and gave the farrier a sharp cuff on the head.

"Fool," he hissed as he loomed over the humbler man. "My best courser lost a shoe, so I've had to cut short my hunt. If you don't fix it and shoe every horse in my stable by the morrow, I'll run *you* down with my hounds."

The farrier emitted a squeak like a frightened rat and set to work with trembling hands and a foul mood. He screamed at his apprentice, who hurried to and fro, working the bellows and trimming hooves. But when the farrier made a crucial error on one of the Lord's palfreys--pricking the sensitive hoof with an ill-struck nail--his temper blazed white-hot.

"Look what you made me do, you little brat!" he screeched, and he ripped the bellows out of his niece's hands and struck her across the temple. The iron tip of the bellows burned hot enough to leave a streak of charred and bloody skin across her face and head, and heavy enough to crack her skull.

It was a miracle Soot did not fall down dead right then. Had the farrier stuck her again, she likely would have. But even the hardest of hearts might hide a speck of softness, and her uncle threw down his bellows and let her be.

How she arrived at Birgitte and Cresputina's doorstep is unknown. Some say she walked there herself, her footsteps guided by providence to the one person who could help her. Some think Cresputina had been watching over her and used her magic to call the girl to the alehouse, transporting her threw the air by witchery. Others think that regret may have softened the farrier's heart enough that he deposited the girl on the alehouse doorstep himself. Whatever the case, Birgitte woke that night to a banging sound on the door, and by the time she'd thrown on her robe and come downstairs, Cresputina was already laying Soot out on the long alehouse table.

"Quickly! I need clean water and fresh linens!" Cresputina said. Birgitte hurried to help, and together they washed poor Soot's wounded head and tried to staunch the bleeding. But already the flesh around the burn had turned dark and swollen, and the blood that seeped from between their fingers smelled sickly-sour. The girl's breathing came in short gasps.

Cresputina had never treated such a wound before. It was one thing to straighten a limb, especially on a day the stars had aligned on the side of healing and renewal. But this child would surely die without powerful magicks, ones she wasn't certain she could control.

Soot moaned and grabbed at her grubby sackcloth. "Too hot," she murmured. Cresputina lifted the girl's rags to cool her down. The marks she saw on the child's flesh made her lips quiver with fury. Bruises, burns, half-healed scars. Ribs jutting out of pale, clammy skin.

She would not allow this girl to die, Cresputina decided, whatever the cost. She mixed healing oils, powders, and herbs in a pot. The salve she made felt cool to the touch and smelled the mint leaves and willow bark, but real magic is not in salves but in a witch's heart. She smoothed the salve on Soot's burn and murmured a spell. The fever-heat abated briefly, then roared back.

It would not do, Cresputina thought, and her heart was troubled. She would have to draw the fire out of the girl's flesh, but fire was tricky to control. It flickers and dances, it consumes all in its path. If even a spark escaped her fingers, who knew what havoc it would create?

119

Cresputina took a deep breath and ran her fingers through Soot's hair. Clumps of it came loose in her hands and fell to the floor, which meant she had to work quickly. She wove the remaining hair into a spiral braid, one that could channel heat away from the girl's wound. Clasping the ends of Soot's hair firmly in her right hand, Cresputina traced her left over the spiral, pulling fire along the braid and channelling it. She hummed a spell, one as wild and changeable as fire itself, trying to direct its heat to safe places--the hearth, the clear cold water Birgitte had brought for her. The swelling around the burn subsided at last, and the wound itself cooled. Hope leapt in the Haar-witch's chest, even as the water next to her began to boil, bubbling and spilling over its bucket.

With the water boiling and the hearth fire raging, Cresputina did not dare to channel more fire into them. She hesitated, and as fire began to build up in Soot's braid, her hair turned a deep and vibrant shade of red, one she had all the days of her life thereafter, even as an old woman.

The ground would be the only other place that could contain such heat, Cresputina decided. She directed the last of the fire into the Earth beneath her feet. It charred a hole in the floorboards, but the cold soil seemed to absorb it well enough. Sweat ran down her face, and her whole body shook from the magics that flowed through her like a rain-swollen river. Once, the river of fire overflowed Cresputina's control, and she felt fire-magic leap off her fingers and dance away. She gritted her teeth grimly, but there was nothing to be done. Birgitte's alehouse had not caught fire yet, so there was that.

Dawn peaked over the horizon by the time Cresputina collapsed on the floor, weak and shaking, as wrung out as one of Birgitte's dishcloths. But just before she fell into a sleep so deep she didn't wake for three days, she heard a chirping voice ask about breakfast. Soot sat up on the table, a halo of fire-red hair floating around her head, and her wound healed as thoroughly as if it had never been.

There are sparks of fire that lodge in dry wood or coals. Other sparks seek the deep earth, where they make molten rocks. A few try to fly up to the sun, a place they feel is their rightful ancestral home. But some prefer to lodge themselves in the hearts of men and women, setting them ablaze with wild passions and fury. These are the most dangerous, for they consume the minds and spirits of their hosts and drive them to strife of all kind.

By some terrible misfortune, or perhaps as the consequence of such powerful magicks, the spark that escaped Cresputina's fingers when she healed Soot was this last kind. It floated through the village of Mont Noire in the early morn, as invisible as a spider's web in the grey light, a tiny flicker smaller than the flame of a guttering candle. Had it found only gentle souls, it's possible it would have just gone out. But that is not what it found.

The spark embedded itself in the local priest, Father Bernard. That night he had a nightmare, and he woke up hot and feverish. Years of austerity and a standoffish belief in his own superiority had desiccated his heart into a bed of dry tinder. The spark set it ablaze with righteous fury, until he rose from his hard bed and knelt at the foot of the cross. Fire purifies, he thought, and the village is full of sin. Why, just the other day he saw the Butcher's wife looking most coquettishly at her husband's apprentice, even though she had a suckling babe! He would purify them all.

The very next day the priest began his crusade in the village square, calling down hellfire and damnation on the women there for their irreverence.

"Women adorn themselves in vanity," he screamed, pointing at a young woman with shining hair spilling out of the braided bands Cresputina had woven across her brow. She shrank away from him, but he gripped her locks in his fists. His face contorted with rage, and perhaps a more carnal emotion, as he loomed over her. She slipped his grasp and fled, sobbing.

"Vain, slovenly wench!" He yelled at her back. "What witch has claimed your soul for the King of Lusts?"

From then on, Father Bernard spent his days railing against the weakness and vanity of women. A few women he bullied into forgoing Cresputina's lovely braids, or undoing ones she'd already woven into their hair. But her styles were so popular that few women went without them very long, especially when they knew about the good spells she worked in their hair. Many women had Cresputina to thank for their husbands' increased affection, or their daughters' happy marriages, or the success of their family's shop on market days.

Yet the paltry attention most villagers gave his crusade only inflamed the priest further. When he could not interest the village women in his quest for purity, chastity, and modesty, he turned to the men. Here he found a bit more success. A few men grumbled that when they went to strike their wives or daughters, as was a man's right in those days, their blows seemed to bounce off and leave the intended recipients unharmed. Others spoke of the uncanny way that Birgitte's daughter had recovered her broken foot. But all of them kept quiet about Cresputina's involvement in these things, accept the old town bailiff.

"Why old John Farrier wept when he told me. Right miracle it was, he said, the little'un coming back with not a mark on her, but her hair turned red as forge-fire. No harm in it, I suppose, but it's darned unnatural," the bailiff told Father Bernard.

"Aye, unnatural. Pray tell, where did the child go? Who was it helped her?" the priest asked.

The bailiff shifted awkwardly. He was a man who liked to hear himself talk and fancied he knew all the goings-on of the village, a point of pride. But he did not like the glint in the priest's eye, an unsavory reflection of the fire that blazed within.

"Some woman or other," he finally answered. "None too important, for truth."

"A woman of power is always important," Father Bernard said. "For women are weak and changeable, and a woman who cures one day will kill the next." He loomed over the old man, and the bright flames in his eyes made the shadows underneath them seem deep and dark.

"Well..." the bailiff said, then stopped. He coughed and looked at the floor.

"I see. Does some misplaced loyalty or devotion strangle your tongue? Has your aged mother been indulging herself with spells and enchantments, or your wife, or--" the priest's eyes widened, and his lips curled into a crooked smile, "your daughter? Didn't I see her just the other day, with twin braids bouncing down her back? They were certainly lovely, and I don't recall seeing her wear them before."

The bailiff tried to swallow the bile that rose in his throat at Father Bernard's insinuations. He had given many confessions to the priest, and the urge to confess pressed on him now.

"She had the spotted fever, and took a turn for the worse, and my wife thought it'd do no harm, sir, none at all, just to have her hair braided like the other girls--"

123

"Of course, my good man, of course you meant well. How many foolish men have been led astray by the witcheries of women? Fear not, fear not, no harm will come to you and yours. At least, not if you tell me who has been doing all this enchantment."

The bailiff plucked at the lacings on his shirt, twisting the leather cords in his hands. A drop of sweat rolled down his cheek, or perhaps a tear.

"It were--it were--" he bit his lip, but words tumbled out of his mouth nonetheless. "It were Cresputina. Her that boards with the widow alewife."

"There now," the priest said. "You have made your confession. It's not so bad, aye? And I will absolve you and your kin for the terrible sin of consorting with that witch. *If* you go to your master and tell him I must speak to him forthwith."

The bailiff's master was the Lord of Dark Mountain, who ruled over Mont Noire and the surrounding villages when he wasn't fighting in the King's wars. He was tall and had broad shoulders knotted with muscle and a bristly black beard. But his heart was cold and capricious, and the peasants lived in great fear of his temper. Father Bernard made his appeal very carefully, hitting just the right notes to stir the Lord's wrath and his eagerness for public executions, of which there had been far too few of late for his taste.

"Have it your way, priest," the Lord said, scratching his beard. "I'll have my men put her in irons. Do you want a trial or should we just build a pyre and roast the wench?"

"She's a foreigner, my Lord, not a citizen. Why waste time on a trial when I have evidence and convincing testimony that she's guilty? Besides, we wouldn't want her to escape, or use her witchery to turn the crowd against us."

"Very well," the Lord said. He summoned his men and bid them arrest Cresputina.

Cresputina herself was still recovering from the powerful magics that she'd drawn on to heal Soot. She had lain in bed for days, shaking and feverish from the leftover heat she'd pull from the girl. A dark foreboding gripped her, and she saw flames all around her and smelled their smoke. Had she made a mistake with the spell? She was afraid to touch anything, lest her fingers set it alight. Birgitte fed her calming broths and her best ales, and her two youngest daughters tip-toed around the house like mice.

The thunder of hooves approaching the alehouse didn't frighten the good widow. She was used to travellers stopping in for a drink and a quick bite. Even the pounding knocks at her door, powerful enough to shake the whole house, could be chalked up to thirsty lords eager for her fare. But Birgitte did not expect to be thrust aside with a gauntleted hand when she let the travelers in. When she opened her mouth to protest, the gauntlet crashed into her face with enough force to knock out some of her teeth. Her daughters froze in their tasks, but Birgitte waved at them, silently imploring them to run. Her youngest snapped out of her shock and grabbed her sister. They skittered away.

But Birgitte did not dare scream a warning to Cresputina, even if she could have gotten words out through her swollen lips. So it was that the Haar-witch was unprepared when soldiers stormed into her room. She was too weak to flee or protest. Her fingers flew to her hair, in hopes that she could weave a braid of protection or hiding before they could get to her, but it was too late. Soldiers grabbed her arms and pinned them to her sides. One of them slammed a fist into her belly. Black spots filled her vision and she hunched over in pain.

Worst of all, Father Bernard had given special instructions to one of the men. He gripped to the Haar-witch's hair, which fell in long dark locks around her bent neck and sawed it off with a sharp knife. Cresputina let out a scream and struggled against the men holding her, but the soldier did not stop. He hacked and cut her black curls until he reached her bare scalp, even leaving great gashes and cuts in her skin.

Cresputina's stomach heaved, and bile spilled out of her mouth. As they dragged her off, she saw them scooping up her shorn strands and throwing them into the hearthfire. Then she fainted dead away.

She woke up on a cold stone floor, her body aching all over. Where had they taken her? It was dark and smelled faintly of rotten grain, so perhaps a storehouse of some kind. She touched the walls on either side of her with her fingertips. She pulled herself up and felt along the walls for the door. Rough wood, perhaps a little aged, but still too solid for her to break down, not without a spell. And she had no hair to draw power from. She ran her hand over her bare scalp. Shorn away--her beauty, her magick, the essence of her craft. They'd burn her at the stake, as they had so many of her kind. Cresputina curled into a ball, covered her face with her hands, and wept.

Father Bernard wasted no time in proclaiming his victory to anyone who'd listen. If a few of the villagers cringed when they heard about Cresputina's arrest, he didn't care. If one or two women had tears leaking out of their eyes when they heard his joyous news, that didn't matter. He'd won. The Lord's men were building a pyre in the town square, and he'd burn the witch the very next Sunday. That was only the beginning. He'd purify the village, purge the women of their vanity and foolishness, and require them to wear only plain, modest hairstyles and clothes. And those who resisted--he'd have pyres for them, too. He made sure to say that to every woman he met, especially those who cried over the witch.

The day of the witch-burning, Father Bernard rang the Matins bright and early. The scent of blooming flowers and fresh-cut hay wafted through the village on a gentle breeze. The pyre had a light coating of dew, but it was not too wet to keep the fire from lighting. The villagers stood in the square, looking huddled and glum despite the lovely Spring weather. Women and girls were not wearing the vibrant kirtles they usually donned on Sundays, but the dark clothes they wore for mourning. The priest approved of their more modest dress.

The Lord's men dragged Cresputina out of the church cellar. They'd stripped off her filthy kirtle, leaving only her long white shift for modesty. The thin linen would burn away almost immediately, she knew, leaving her naked and writhing in the fire, bound to the stake. Part of the entertainment, she thought, shivering. She hadn't eaten in over a week, which made her feel thin and insubstantial, like ashes that might blow away on the wind. She wondered if there was any hope of escape as they bound her to the pyre with heavy ropes. Alas, she thought, looking at the priest. She'd never charm him--he was too bald.

She looked out over the crowd of villagers. At least they weren't throwing dung and offal at her or screaming obscenities. The village women were silent as the grave, and the men murmured quietly. Gwaine, the butcher's apprentice, frowned at the priest, and Birgitte's young son-in-law was shaking his head, his arm wrapped protectively around his wife.

Only one person was openly weeping. That was Soot, who stood at the base of the pyre with tears streaming down her face.

Father Bernard pushed her out of the way to deliver his sermon, a burning torch in his hand.

The villagers could hear little of the priest's speech above Soot's sobs, apart from shrill screeches of "Modesty!" or "Vile Vanity!" He thought his words were having the desired effect. Why, after his screed against the immorality of women's adornment, which ignited the unholy lusts of men, the farrier's girl took out her belt knife, hacked off her vivid red locks, and laid them on the pyre by the witch's feet. The girl was weeping, that's true, but perhaps she only cried in shame at her terrible sinfulness.

After that, women approached the pyre, one by one. They cut off braids and flowing hair, lover's knots and elegant coiled twists, some still scented with Cresputina's oils and powers. If a few men shifted uncomfortably, disturbed by the loss of so much of the town's beauty, they did not intervene to stop their wives or daughters from shearing away their lovely hair. By the end of the sermon, an abundant pile of hair lay at Cresputina's feet, silver and white entwined with gold and black and fire-red, shining and beautiful. For the first time, the witch's eyes grew wet, and Father Bernard's heart softened a bit. The witch could see how the village women were rejecting her sinful wares, he thought. That might be enough to make her repent in time to suffer the torments of purgatory, instead of being condemned to hell forevermore.

With a wave of his hand, Father Bernard lit the pyre. But it did not react the way he intended. The fire did not burn red and orange, as fires ought, nor did it smell of smoke and burnt flesh as expected. Instead, it crackled and sparkled in brilliant hues of pink and green, and the scent of fresh flowers and myrrh filled the air. Many of the villagers wept now, and when he turned to see the witch wriggling and struggling in torment in the flames, she was not there. The ropes had fallen away, and the woman floated above the billowing white smoke, her body as wispy and transparent as a sylph's. She hovered over the village women who'd shorn their hair for her, touching each one on the head with ethereal hands. Then quick as the spring breeze, she was gone.

After the fire burned down, men searched the ashes, but they could find no bones. The priest locked himself in the chantry, and villagers heard him weeping and scourging himself. When he would not come out after a number of days, they sent to the bishop, who had him brought to a monastery where he could spend his days in solitude and contemplation. The new priest who came to Mont Noire was a gentle sort, happy to bless all he met, from high lords to barefoot children.

No one saw Cresputina again, but stories about her spread for miles around. And the women and girls of Mont Noire became renowned for the beauty of their hair, so thick and vibrant and lustrous, so lovely it looks imbued with magic even today.

Lantgen

BLOOD SAUSAGE, SALT PORK

It was not often, Nikolas thought, that he found himself investigating rumors of child-stealing demons in the remote villages of the empire. It was even less often that the respected envoy and religious counselor of the Great Emperor Flavius Valerius Aurelius Constantinus Augustus found himself at the mercy of a recalcitrant mule. But the mule had the stubbornness of Doubting Thomas and the road had all the pitfalls marshy sand and years of neglect could bestow. Nik had endured a great many hardships, including time in the previous Emperor's prisons, but this trip had become one of the worst experiences of his life.

"It's not that far to the village," he said to the stubborn horse-beast God had punished him with. "I will make sure they feed you the best grains, oats and rye the like of which you have never seen."

The beast gave Nik a doleful look, clearly pitying its master's stupidity.

131

"Well, perhaps the grain is half-molded, but surely it's better to spend the night in a warm stable than out here alone on the road. We could be robbed or catch our death of cold!"

The beast cocked its head and gave a soft whinny-haw sound.

"Fine, stay here then. Maybe you'll make a delicious pot of stew for a band of robbers! Or the demon the villagers say is prowling around."

Nik swore he heard the mule mutter a curse, a sound no natural horse-beast could make. Then it gave him a last grudging look and started stomping along the road. Nik sighed. He had no strong desire to reach the village either; it was the source of such dark and unholy rumors a wise man would stay well clear of the place.

"I'm not as wise as I should be," he said aloud, though no one could hear him except the mule, or perhaps God. The horse-beast whinny-hawed in agreement.

The village had an evil smell, a horrid combination of rotted meat, filth, and a sickly marsh-scent. A warren of cottages and shops clustered near the road, with one or two small insulae for salt miners. There was a tiny temple to Zeus that had been repurposed as a Christian church, a single inn, and one small domus which was probably the home of the village praetor or lesser official of some sort.

All told, it was not as bad as he'd expected for a place preyed upon by a fiendish murderer. In fact, it was better off than many of the other villages Nik had passed, which had been burned to rubble in the civil strife under the old Emperor.

"Should I go to the praetor first? Or should I ask at the church?" Nik asked the mule. The beast whinny-hawed and headed toward the domus. Nik followed it, digging through his bags for his Bishop's mitre. The ridiculous hat would brush the ceilings of any building in the town, but it had a most remarkable effect on villagers, who granted him generous guest-rights when he wore it.

He knocked at the domus' door. An elderly woman opened it. He bowed, though she wore the plain clothes of a servant. She eyed his hat before inviting him in.

"Dominus! There's a funny fellow with a fancy hat at the door!" she yelled. A young man stumbled into the hall, looking rather drunk.

"That is indeed a fancy hat," he said. "You must be important!"

Nik bowed, careful to keep the mitre from slipping off his head as it was wanting to do. "The Great Emperor Constantinus Augustus sent me to aid you in driving out that demon which is stealing your children."

"He did?" The praetor said.

Nik sighed. "Yes."

The praetor blinked. "Well then you may have guest-rights in my domus. Come in, we'll open an amphora. The wine from around here tastes like swamp-sludge, but my uncle in Corinth sends me his best."

"I would be grateful, dominus," Nik replied.

The praetor, whose name was Acrisius, called for food. The old woman brought out a platter of olives, mashed chickpeas, local vegetables, and a hard, buttery cheese, as well as a jug of olive oil and some warm flat bread. Simple, delicious fare.

"You are lucky to drink such excellent wine," Nik said. He nodded graciously, and the elderly servant poured him another cup.

"Indeed!" the praetor said. "Let us drink to the emperor's health and goodwill!"

That night they made a good many toasts to the Emperor's health and goodwill, though so far as Nik knew Constantine was quite robust and generally well disposed. But he believed in the principle of "in vino veritas" when dealing with local bureaucrats. Unfortunately, he learned that while Praetor Acrisius might be truthful under the influence of his uncle's wine, he was not very knowledgeable about the village he commanded. In fact, Nik concluded that the youth had little knowledge of any subject at all. Still, it never hurt to ask.

"How many children have gone missing thus far?"

"Who knows?" Acrisius said. "They run away as soon as they come of age to avoid the salt mines. I can hardly keep enough little buggers in town to keep them running. Even the slaves never last longer than a few months before they run away. Or die. Cave-ins, you know. Constantly getting crushed down there."

Nik suppressed a shudder. "And the ones that were found?"

The praetor fingered a pagan amulet around his neck, then hastily crossed himself. "Strigoi," he whispered. "The priest found the bones. They'd been broken open, and the marrow sucked out. I had the villagers dig up anyone who'd died recently and burn the bodies."

"And did the disappearances stop?"

"We found no more bodies," Acrisius said with a shrug. "But three more children disappeared from the mines."

Nik frowned. He did not believe in strigoi, which were old pagan tales. In his experience, most folk who took to cannibalism were starving, not cursed. He'd seen it before during the great famine. Nonetheless, it would not hurt to inquire about the praetor's tale. In the morning, after a good night's rest. *And* a visit to the baths.

"I'll speak to your local priest about this strigoi on the morrow, but tonight I believe it is time for me to retire. It was a long journey."

The old woman showed Nik to the baths. She gave him a toothless grin and pressed a cake of soap into his hand. It had a strange marking etched on it: a woman holding two torches flanked by a pack of dogs.

"If I was to go looking for missing kids," she said. "I wouldn't talk to that ninny priest. I'd ask that brazen hussy." She turned before he could ask any more questions and hobbled down the hall.

Nikolas woke the next day stiff and aching from riding the thrice-damned mule-demon, his head pounding from too much wine. He pulled on a battered black cassock and said his morning prayers. He felt he'd need a great deal of grace to make it through the day.

The village was as woe-begotten in the morning light as it had been the evening before. The sun's heat seemed to have cooked the foul smells of the swamp into an even more revolting stew.

He went to the converted temple-church, a sad little building whose mosaics had crumbled into bits of broken ceramics. Deep gouges marred its thick wooden doors, and the cross on its eaves was lopsided. Nik wondered if it had been attacked during the civil wars or if it had been stripped of pagan artwork by peasants with more fervor than skill.

Before he could knock, the church doors burst open.

"Your Grace!" exclaimed the local priest. He bobbed at Nik. His tonsured head shined with sweat and his cassock smelled like ripe cheese.

135

"I am pleased to meet you, Reverend Father," Nik said.

"Oh, I'm so glad you've come! And from the great city of Constantine! I have been much put upon here, much put upon. Why, the widow--"

"Father, the Praetor informed me that you found the bones from the strigoi attack. Where are they now?"

"Oh, fear not, fear not, I gave them a proper burial, and we performed rites to sanctify the church and its surroundings. I'm sure the demon is gone--"

Nik raised his hand. "I must see the bones and their crypt to complete my inquiries."

"As you say, your grace. Everything was done proper, though we could not tell who the poor victim was. To prevent them from rising I buried them beneath the reliquary of Saint Stephen, martyred not far from here by--"

"I should pray over the remains, alone. Perhaps God will send me a vision."

"Yes, yes, of course." The priest led him to a corner of the church, where there was a small marker stone set beneath a wooden reliquary box painted with a clumsy portrait of St. Stephen. The priest fervently crossed himself as they approached the grave, then mumbled an excuse and bustled out the door. Nik sighed with relief.

He took out a small pouch of red powder he kept hidden in his cassock and mixed it with holy water to make a paste. He dabbed a dot of the paste on the reliquary, then on the victim's gravestone. Next, he smeared some on his forehead and above his heart. Finally, with only a little cringing, he poured the rest in his mouth. It tasted like ashes mixed with horse piss, and his eyes watered. But already his other senses began to wake.

He caught no scent of magic from the bones, and none of the lingering sulfur-smell he might expect from a demon. But there was an unusual perfume--a bit of exotic spice, such as he had not smelled since he returned from Damascus. And the thick, acrid scent of salt, so heavy he wondered if the victim had been one of the miners. The bones were small, but the praetor said even young children worked in the mines.

He pulled his mitre low over his forehead to hide the red stain from the paste, then left the church. The swamp smell overwhelmed his senses, and Nik swayed on his feet. But his mind snapped back to the spice. Very few in a town like this could afford fine spice. He followed the scent trail passed the villagers' hovels and the praetor's domus. On the edge of town, along a short, treacherous path through thick, sandy mud, he found a ruined domus, half buried in the swamp. It had a roof though and looked habitable if a person could overlook the slanted walls. He knocked. Red paint flaked off beneath his knuckle.

The woman who opened the door had long hair the rich, earthy color of a fresh tilled field. She had the perfect features of an angel but for the sensual smile that played across her lips. Her eyes opened wide as she looked him, then she seemed to laugh to herself.

"I did not think a bishop would partake in the services I offer, but all men are welcome here, your Grace."

Nik felt his heart stutter. A hetaera. Her perfume had the exotic, spice smell he remembered from the bazaars of Damascus, but beneath it he could smell her, heady and rich. A hunger stirred in his body that he hadn't felt since before his vows. She leaned towards him, letting her robe fall open. Blood rushed in his veins.

He shook himself, stepping back. He doffed his mitre and bowed.

"Good lady, I'm here at the Emperor's behest, to investigate the disappearances and murders this town has suffered." Good lord, he thought, inwardly cringing. I sound like a pompous ass.

She pulled her robe closed, though not before he caught a glimpse of bare skin, pink and flushed.

"I am Cassia of Antioch, your grace," she said. "Come in."

"What brings a woman like you to a tiny provincial village?" Nik asked. He tried not to notice the way her robe slid over the curves of her body. She had crammed a long couch in the atrium, one richly draped with silk coverlets and pillows. She sat with him on the couch, so close that with his heightened senses he could hear her heart beating and smell the sweet, salt tang of her skin. He swallowed.

She laughed. "A woman must have her mysteries. I took up a wandering life long ago, and it suits me."

"But Antioch is a Christian city, and surely no one there would..."

"Sell their daughter's virtue? Why not? Even Christ loved the Magdalene, they say."

"Did you know the child?" he asked. "The one they say was killed by a strigoi?"

She paused, and her scent took on the bittersweetness he associated with liars. "No, of course not. I do not take children as apprentices."

"Perhaps one of the village boys took to following you around, as boys are want? Did one come to you?" Nik asked.

"I do not take boys as patrons, either," she said. "I prefer men."

She moved closer to him, so close he could feel the silk of her robe brushing on his hand, and his face grew hot. He wanted

138

to pray "God give me the strength to resist temptation!" But he did not. He did not trust his heart. Instead, he stood up, holding his arms in front of him as if he had forgotten what to do with them. He looked her in the eye, then decided that was a bad idea and looked away again.

"You're lying," Nik said. But before he could think of anything else to say, her lips touched his, and he felt the soft curves of her body press against him. Her kiss intoxicated him, her spicy, earthy scent like hunger and heat. Her robe fell open. His hands found bare skin, flushed and rosy.

"Christe," he whispered. "Christe, eleison..." It was enough--his mind cleared, at least a little. He backed away from her, tripping over a particularly fine silk carpet.

"I... uh...that is, I must be going," Nik said from his awkward position on her floor. He scrambled up and out the door, trying very hard not to hear the sweet, bell-like voice calling after him.

"So, you met Cassia," Acrisius said. "I'd know that look anywhere."

Nik didn't answer but flushed a telltale crimson.

"She's not bad, you know, as those sorts of women go. When she and her brother first arrived, I considered having her arrested, but, well, she's done wonders for the morale of this cursed place."

No doubt, Nik thought. And she likely paid her local taxes in service to you. An image rose in his mind of Acrisius, drunk, thrusting into the hetaera with all the tenderness of a man spearing wild boar in the hunt. No wonder Christ had so much compassion for the Magdalene. He felt slightly sick.

"She told me she was from Antioch," Nik said. "And she has a brother as well?"

"Yes, he's the local butcher. They came here after the war. Their father went bankrupt, so his family was auctioned into slavery to pay his debts. Her brother was bought by a slaughterhouse, but Emperor Maximian bought Cassia. Towards the end of his life you know, the old Emperor came to believe the blood of virgins would keep him young. They say he took her maidenhead that very night, though she was but nine years old."

Nik took a gulp of wine. "And have either of them ought to do with this mysterious strigoi?"

Acrisius laughed. "My maidservant would have me string them both up by their thumbs. She thinks the butcher is stealing children for their meat, but that's servant nonsense. Cassia could make more money in one night than they'd earn selling all the wretched brats in town to the sultans of the East."

There was a sniff from the corner, where the elderly servant busied herself spinning coarse swamp flax. Nik saw her make a sign with her fingers to avert the evil eye.

"I should meet this butcher," he said. He felt as though the ground beneath his feet had lurched, as though he was standing on the shifting desert sands of the Holy Land. He stared into his wine cup, as though the answers he sought lay within its depths.

Nik sought the butcher early the next morning before most of the village had roused itself. The man was younger than Nik had expected, with a wispy brown beard and pale skin. He had a haunted, twitchy look, as though he was lost in dreams, none of them pleasant. He worked outside his shop, chopping dark red meat.

"What are you preparing?" Nik asked.

"Sausages, your Grace," the butcher replied in a tremulous whisper. He sprinkled the meat with salt and herbs.

"Many of the children in your village have disappeared or been murdered, and I am here to find what is happening. Did you know any of the missing children?"

"No," the butcher whispered, so softly Nik could barely hear his voice. Behind him, he heard angry mutters. The village was waking, and though the butcher's shop was located on a main thoroughfare, villagers gave it a wide berth. Older women shot furious glares at them and made the sign against evil. The butcher's hands began to tremble.

"I must tend to things in the shop," he said.

One of the villagers hissed and spat on the ground near the butcher's block, and the young man flinched as though he'd been struck. He hurriedly gathered the seasoned meat in a bowl and fled inside his shop.

"Go and hide, Simon Child-Thief!" an elderly man called after him.

"Strigoi," hissed another.

Nik frowned. He had not taken the red powder this morning, afraid that he'd be unable to resist Cassia's tempting scent under its influence, but some of its effects still lingered. The village had the tense, sulfuric smell of an oncoming storm, and the villagers moved like hissing cats. He followed the butcher.

"Wait!" Nik called. He stopped short. He heard strange noises behind the door--a choked scream, then a high voice, panicked--a child.

Maybe he is a child-thief, Nik thought. He knocked hard on the butcher's door.

"Open, in the name of the Emperor and his church!"

The door creaked, and a tiny face peeked out--a girl, thin as a rail, with long dark hair.

"Please help!" she whispered, beckoning. He followed her inside.

The shop was dark but clean, with none of the rotten-meat smell Nik had expected. Dried sausages hung in neat rows, entwined with bulbs of hanging garlic. Huge salt barrels took up most of the floor. Nik squeezed his way through them to follow the girl. He found her leaned over the butcher's crumpled form.

"He's been cursed," she whispered. "The shaking takes him, and he falls down. He tries not to let us see, but the strigoi cursed him!"

Nik knelt by the butcher and rolled the man onto his side. He had a few herbs that might treat convulsions, but Simon was too deep in the fit to safely swallow them. Instead he prayed quietly. After a short time, the convulsions stopped, and the butcher fell into a deep sleep. Nik watched and waited. The girl sobbed.

The butcher awoke looking confused. "Where am I? Theodora? Don't cry, little one, I'm sorry if I scared you..."

"There are other things you should be sorry for, Simon Butcher," Nik said. "Lying to a man of God and the Emperor's representative, for one."

"Emperor? Humph. Murderers and monsters, the whole lot of 'em. If you'd seen how the last one treated Cassia, you'd never brag about serving one of them." The butcher's tone was fierce, but his voice weak, barely more than a whisper.

Nik didn't answer. Truth be told, he himself had spent time in Maximian's dungeons, but Constantine seemed well enough, as such men went.

"But what of you? A child-thief? Why are you keeping this girl here? Who are her people?" Nik asked.

Theodora's thin, pale face twisted into a fierce glare, and she spat on the ground by his feet.

"What do you know of it? Simon and Cassia saved me and the others! My mam sold me to the mines! I worked in the damp and dark and salt for weeks until Simon broke my chains! It's not his fault about the strigoi!"

Nik raised his eyebrows. "Does Theodora speak truth, Simon Butcher?" he asked.

"Aye," the butcher said. He looked ill and shaky. "It was Cassia's idea. Once we had enough income, we could set other children free. Keep them from suffering like we did. She'd tear down the child brothels with her bare hands if she could."

Nik sighed and closed his eyes in silent prayer. He hated slavery, especially child slavery. He'd once used a large donation to pay the dowries of all the poor girls in his congregation, to keep their parents from selling them to brothels. For which his confessor had demanded a significant penance.

"What about the child who died? I know Cassia was there. God gave me a vision that lead me to her." Which was true enough, and an explanation most peasants found satisfactory.

"A curse," Simon whispered. "It follows us. A monster. It feeds on the children."

"I told Basil not to wander outside," Theodora said. "We're supposed to stay inside near the salt barrels. But he wanted to catch frogs in the marsh."

"We found him too late. God rest his soul." Simon crossed himself, his hands shaking. "What else could we do? We do not know how to fight a monster. We could only pray for him."

"And God heard your prayers," Nik said. "That is why he sent me."

In truth, Nik had never encountered a strigoi before, and he had only dim ideas on how he might draw one out or find its lair. But if the strigoi was following Cassia and Simon, then it must have a connection to them. Or most likely, to her, as Nik doubted the simple butcher had ever met anyone powerful enough to have become a strigoi.

He needed to talk to Cassia again, although he felt terrible temptations of the flesh around her. He supposed he should dread seeing her. But he could not deny that he deeply desired to see her, talk to her, understand her. A woman who would tear down brothel walls with her bare hands and free the slaves within. A woman who had not let fate make her bitter or cruel but kept her compassion and a will to help others. He desired her, and now he admired her character as well.

He probably should have gone to see her in the morning, instead of seeking her out that evening.

There was another man inside her domus. He heard their voices before he could knock on the door. Raised, angry voices.

"Do you think I'm stupid? I could have you stripped and flogged through the streets," a man's voice yelled.

Cassia spoke, but her voice was too low for Nik to make out her words. The man laughed.

"Maybe for now. But he won't stop the villagers from burning your brother's shop to the ground, if they get restive. Oh yes, I know something about that! Stay away from the boys. If any more of them go missing or manage to slip their bonds, I'll light torches for the bonfire myself!"

The door flew open. A burly man in a salt stained tunic strode passed Nik without a word. Nik watched him go. He had a hard face, rough and leathery like an over-cured hide.

The scent of exotic spice. A soft hand on his shoulder.

"Don't trouble yourself about him," Cassia said, her voice soothing and warm as slipping into a tepidarium. Nik had clenched his fists when he heard the rough man threaten Cassia, but he relaxed them now. A foolish display would not help anyone.

"I spoke to your brother," he said. Her fingers traced the skin on his neck, her touch gentle and intoxicating. He turned to look in her eyes, which were as dark and fathomless as the night sky. "And to Theodora, the slave you helped escape."

Her fingers paused over his flesh, but her expression stayed the same except for a flicker in the depths of her eyes. Her lips parted softly.

"What do you want?" she asked. "To protect the girl and keep our secret? I can offer you...anything. Everything I have to give."

"No!" The word burst from him. She pulled back in shock, her face a mask of fear.

"No," Nik said, softer this time. "That is not what I meant. I would not--that is not what I--your secret, Theodora's secret, is safe with me. I would not betray you or her, you don't need to..."

Cassia gave him a sharp, searching look. "Then why are you here?" she asked.

"I want to stop the strigoi," he said. "And I think you can help me."

She raised an eyebrow. "Come inside."

"I have been with many men. Some are good, some are cruel. Most are simply lustful fools." Cassia filled two fine silver goblets with wine, mixing each one lightly with water. She handed him a goblet. "Only one was a terror." She made a sign to avert evil with her fingers.

"Not just to me or the other girls, you know. He burnt a church full of martyrs and killed tens of thousands. And he betrayed Constantine Augustus and lead a rebellion." She stared into the depths of her cup.

"He had cast me aside by then," she continued. "I was relieved to have survived. Other girls--ones I'd grown close to--had not. When he was captured by the Emperor, he was found with the body of the girl who'd been kindest to me, who'd protected me. Calliope. She sang beautifully, like the muse she'd been named for. I heard later that Constantine was so disgusted with him he'd issued a damnatio memoriae. Even speaking his name was forbidden. So, I don't speak it. Instead, I try to honor her, Calliope. I try to find other children like us and set them free."

"And the strigoi?" Nik asked.

Cassia's lips trembled. "He killed himself before his trial. So much evil in his life, then an unclean death. What else could create such a monster?"

"We have to find him to destroy him. I will need your help."

Cassia closed her eyes and pressed her forehead to the smooth silver of the goblet in her hand.

"The strigoi," she said after a long while, "it's dangerous. Even if I could lure him out or help you find him, what then? How do you kill something that has died once already?"

They fell silent. Nik remembered his first encounter with a demonic creature. A voice in the desert and shadowy images in the corners of his eyes--they'd nearly driven him mad. Brother Crispus had bound his wrists with silver and anointed him with sacred oils. In the morning all the brothers in the monastery had gone looking for the beast. Only Nik was found alive.

"I have not killed a strigoi," Nik said. "But I have heard stories about how it is done. You must cut out the heart and feed it to the demon's victims. I've heard other methods, but destroying the heart is crucial."

"That's if we can even find him," Cassia said. "Simon went looking once, after... he found nothing, though perhaps that was a blessing."

Nik took a sip of wine. He wanted to pat her arm or even put his arm around her for comfort, but he did not want her to misunderstand his intention. Instead, he pulled out a small flask he had hidden in his cassock. When he opened it, the scent from the flask was strong, sharp, and unpleasantly fishy, like cheap garum mixed with garlic. Cassia wrinkled her nose.

"It's pungent," Nik said. "I made it today. If we drink enough of it--"

"Oh no," Cassia said. "You intend for us to drink that?"

"Unfortunately. It will not hurt us, though I am told it can cause ill humors in the stomach."

"What does it do?"

Nik stroked his beard. "He has a connection to you. That connection might be powerful enough to call him into your dreams."

Cassia shuddered. "Into my nightmares."

"You would not face him alone. If we are together, and--" he blushed. "If our flesh touches, I should be able to enter the dream with you."

147

That would be important, he knew. The horrors of the past are strong in dreams, and dangerous. He doubted either of them could survive alone. Nik sighed. He had ink stained nails and the long nimble fingers of a scholar. He had never wielded a sword or born a shield, and he could not kill the monster in a physical fight. But the other way, the way of the mind, had its dangers as well.

Cassia's fingers strayed a necklace she wore, an Egyptian design of a bird in flight, made of pure gold. It was beautiful-- each feather seemed soft and lifelike, as though it might breathe at any moment, or launch itself into the sky. As she touched it, Cassia stopped shuddering and squared her shoulders.

"I will do it," she said. "Even if I must drink that horrid concoction you've brought, which is stinking up my domus." She tossed her hair. "Customers will complain, you know. I will lose business."

"Will you?" Nik said. "How unfortunate."

He could tell when the potion began to take effect. They had not fallen asleep yet, though his eyelids felt heavy. She lay next him, her silks brushing his arm. Her hand was in his, warm and soft. He heard her breathing become ragged and saw wetness on her face. He couldn't bear it, seeing her hurt. He put his arms around her. She leaned into him, her shivering giving way to sleep. He closed his eyes. She felt right in his arms, like a piece of his life he'd missed until then. He sighed, then drifted off.

He woke in the dream. It was dark. Mist flowed over black earth and grey stone cairns. There was a child curled up at the foot of an ancient moss-covered boulder. Her face was painted, and her gown was an obscene parody of a child's dress, flimsy and sheer. Her skin was mottled blue and white, and she shivered in her sleep. He took off his cloak and wrapped it around her. Her eyes flickered open.

"Priest?" she asked. "Is that you?" He knew the girl's voice-- Cassia, as she'd dreamed herself.

"You don't look like a priest," she said slowly. "Not anymore."

He looked down. He had dreamed himself in the rough brown robes he'd worn on pilgrimage. They were coated in a thick layer of sandy dust, just they had been back then.

"I'm a pilgrim today," Nik said. He extended his hand to her. As she stood up, she lengthened into an adult and her dress became a sophisticated golden tunic, bright and shining as armor. She took his hand with cool grace.

"We should set the lure," Cassia said.

"What do you think will draw him?"

"Vulnerability. And blood." She took a shuddering breath.

"Wait," Nik said. "You're frightened. He can use your fear against you and trap you here. Perhaps we should try again another time or find a different lure."

Cassia stared at him, pity and resignation on her face. "Fear is what draws him, what calls to him. I've always known that. And for the rest--it's what I must do. For those he'll hurt in the future if I don't. And for those who he hurt in the past." She closed her eyes.

"We might only get one chance, priest," she said. "We must make the most of it."

Nik blinked, and they were in a lavishly decorated room. There were fine silk couches and an intricate floor mosaic depicting mythical beasts frolicking. Fine vases overflowed with flowers and ripe fruits, and a glowing brazier gave off comforting warmth.

But the beautiful room made Nik profoundly uneasy. The mosaic, he thought. The fanciful creatures grew cruel and frightening the more he looked at them, their tiles tinged with red. The wrought iron tools by the brazier were sharp and perhaps not meant for toasting bread after all. He looked around for Cassia. She lay on one of the couches, a child again, seemingly asleep. But this time she wore tattered rags and heavy manacle around her neck. There was a half-eaten apple in her hand.

"Don't be afraid," the girl said. The manacle bit into her flesh. She tugged it to one side, exposing soft white skin. There was a sharp knife in her hand.

"I need you to do it," she said. "My hands are too slippery; I might cut too deep."

"Do we have too?" he asked. The knife was in his hand, though he didn't remember taking it. It was silver, as wicked and beautiful as the mosaic.

"Blood calls to him. He'll come for it."

He lifted his hand. His fingers found the throbbing pulse of her throat. Not there, he thought. That would kill her. A scratch, then, a deep one, just to the side of the pulse beneath his fingers. The knife moved fast, and blood ran down her throat. So red, he thought, like the juice of a ripe pomegranate.

"Cassia? Are you okay?"

"Hide, priest," she whispered.

He crouched low, and he was a child again, too. Soldiers marched along the road to his village, their armor bright in the sunlight. He lay hidden in the underbrush, watching them. He heard screams in the distance. He needed to get back to his village, to warn the others before it was too late. But it was too late already.

A girl slipped her hand in his.

"Come back to me," she said, and he trusted her though he'd forgotten why. They slipped away into the underbrush and emerged in the beautiful room. The girl slipped back to the couch, blood pooling in her steps. Nik was still a child, as scrawny and reedy as he'd been then. He crawled beneath the couch. From there he could still reach up to hold her hand.

Someone was coming. A man, tall and heavy, dressed in a purple tunic encrusted with golden embroidery. Heavy footsteps echoed through the room.

Nik froze. It was not a man at all, but a corpse, swollen and putrid. Red eyes that burned with hate. It leaned in to the splatters of Cassia's blood, nostrils flaring. It had blue black fingers that split and oozed like rotted sausages. It dipped them in blood and licked them clean.

"Couldn't stay away, little slave? Did you come back for more rutting?" Rasping and deep, the voice was a sound torn from of Hades, yet its speech had the refined inflections of an educated and cultured man. Nik heard Cassia's breath quicken. The man, the beast, the thing moved faster than Nik could imagine for something that heavy. A hand lashed out and clasped one of Cassia's ankles, digging cracked yellow nails into her skin. It yanked her towards him. She screamed.

"Did you come to plead for others, as you did once before? Even then I was unmoved by your mewling. But perhaps I can show you mercy. I promise you, when I'm done and satisfied, if you beg hard enough, I'll let you die."

Cassia twisted and screamed again. The sound tore at Nik. Am I afraid of death? he thought, willing himself to move. He would die here. But he would die with the grace of the martyrs.

The silver knife was in his hand, a pathetic weapon, small and feeble. But he held it as once the archangel held the sword of hosts. He summoned his courage and darted from beneath the couch. He stabbed at the thing with all his strength. The beast had been wrestling with Cassia. It dropped her and screeched. Filthy black gore dripped from a wound in its belly, giving off a foul smell. It lashed out with its long nails, raking Cassia's cheek.

Nik struck again. He was not a child anymore but a young man, a warrior of God. The silver knife opened a stinking wound in the beast's chest. It shrieked. Cold hands enveloped Nik's throat before he could move.

"Once I could have ordered you skinned alive," the thing whispered. "I could have watched each strip peeled away as you howled." It dug its jagged nails into Nik's neck. Nik kicked at the corpse. He clawed at the hands choking him. Blood red eyes, demon eyes, locked him into their gaze. He struggled for breath and black spots drifted across his vision.

A golden woman, a warrior from the legions of Saint Michael, swam before his eyes. Cassia had become an angel. She had the silver knife, but in her hands, it grew into a sword, bright and gleaming. She brought it down on the strigoi's head. It shrieked. Slimy gore spilled out of its skull. It dropped Nik and hurled itself at her.

There was a clang and the screech of metal bending and scraping. The angel Cassia had fallen, and she struggled to get up. The beast had pinned her, and now it dragged its swollen, black tongue over her face. She shuddered and tried to raise her sword, but the strigoi caught her wrist. There was a sickening crunch, and the silver sword clattered to the floor.

Nik felt ill. The dark spots in his vision gave a sickening lurch. He groped around, searching for a way to help her. The strigoi had the silver sword, and he held it like a trained soldier. Nik was no warrior of God, only a humble priest with a few herbs and magic tricks he'd picked up from an old Sibyl long ago. His fingers closed around something heavy and metallic. A thick chain, with manacles, the one that had held Cassia. He gripped it.

The strigoi knelt over Cassia, slicing off her armor, laughing even as its blood splattered across her face. Its blackened lips twisted into a leer. Nik met her eyes, and she nodded. He struggled to his feet.

The strigoi turned as if to look back at him, but Cassia screamed and struggled, drawing its attention. Nik crept behind it, the chain clenched in his fists. He snapped the manacle around the demon's neck. It clanged shut. Nik pulled on the chain, jerking the demon back. It gave a guttural grunt. Cassia kicked and faught, throwing it off her.

Nik lunged at the silver sword while the demon looked unsteady. The demon slashed at him, and Nik felt the edge of the sword slice his belly. He clutched his wound and blood seeped through his fingers.

The strigoi smiled at him and licked its lips. It raised the sword. Behind it, Cassia griped the chain and jerked it back, straining and pulling with all her might. The strigoi howled.

Nik threw himself at the beast. The sword clattered to the ground, but the beast dug its claws into Nik. It lifted him, and Nik's feet kicked the air. Fangs tore into his neck. Nik screamed.

The beast dropped him. Its chest was split, the silver sword sunk deep into its torso. It fell to its knees, then toppled over. Cassia stood behind it.

"Priest!" she cried. She rushed to Nik and knelt by his side, trying to stanch the blood.

Nik wanted to tell her not to worry. He had known the risks. He would not go to God with cowardice staining his soul. He would be a martyr. He had no regrets. Except--he could not speak. He wanted her to know he loved her. Her bravery, her compassion. His heart swelled with it. Her face would be the last thing he would see.

"No," she whispered. "No, there must be a way." She reached into the beast's chest, slicing at something. The heart of a strigoi.

He wanted to tell her no. He wasn't sure what the effects would be. But he could not talk, and even if he could, in that moment he could deny her nothing. She pressed something into his mouth, something raw and slimy. He swallowed.

"Priest? Did it work? Can you hear me?"

Cassia, he thought. His vision dimmed, and her voice sounded far away. Then he knew no more.

He woke in the dark. He groped around him. Soft silk, warm skin, the gentle sound of breath. He did not know where he was, but Cassia was beside him, and he was not afraid. He closed his eyes and drifted away.

Nik's body ached. He heard voices around him. The praetor...Acrisius. Cassia. His eyes flickered open.

"Don't try to move," Cassia said.

"The strigoi, is it--is he--"

"There have been no more attacks," Acrisius said. "But we cannot find the beast's lair to confirm its death."

"I know where it is," Nik said. And he did. Cassia had fed him a piece of the demon's heart, and he could feel where it was now, deep in his bones. "We can go there now, if it pleases you, dominus."

"Your injuries--" Cassia protested.

Nik sat up slowly, testing his strength. "How long have I slept?"

"Only a few days," Acrisius said. "In truth, I expected you to sooner die than wake. But here you are. Perhaps the Christian God does look after his own."

Nik pressed his fingers to his throat and belly. There were still injuries there, but they had healed remarkably fast. Had he been protected in the dream, or did the heart's blood of a strigoi have some powerful virtue?

"Thanks be to God," Nik said. "But I am ready to search the strigoi's lair. It is best we go soon, while it is daylight and the demon sleeps like one dead."

"As you wish," Acrisius said. He waved an ornate gladius. "I will accompany you, and Cassia has determined to go as well."

Nik lead them through the swamp, his sense telling him unerringly where the demon slept. An ancient barrow, a few miles from the salt mines. It had an archway inscribed with worn pagan symbols, one of which Nik recognized—a woman holding two torches, flanked by a pack of dogs.

Acrisius sucked in his breath. "A sanctuary of Hecate. I heard rumors that some still left offerings to the ancient one, but I did not know she had such a presence here."

Nik lead them under the arch and into a dank cave. They moved so silently he could hear water rushing in the depths of the cave. Like the underworld, he thought, with the river Styx. The pagans loved their symbolism--this place would have appealed to them. He wondered who among the villagers gathered here for sacred rites on moonless nights, and if any of them knew about the strigoi. Or had they been his first victims?

The cave opened into large natural cavern. Crystalline stalactites hung from the cave ceiling, and thin slivers of sunlight peeked through cracks. The air smelled of salt.

If Nik had expected an elaborate sarcophagus like Egyptians built in Alexandria, he was disappointed. There was only a large chest, the type soldiers used to carry weapons and provisions, and three salt barrels.

Cassia moved towards a barrel and lifted its lid. She shuddered and turned away.

"What is it?" Nik asked.

"A child," she said. "One of the missing miners."

"The chest," Acrisius said. He fidgeted with his gladius, pulling it out of its scabbard and holding it more like a wine goblet than a sword.

Nik approached the chest. He pulled a small flask of sanctified water out of his cassock and added a few sprinkles of silver dust, then gave it to Cassia.

"Strigoi should be dormant at this hour, but just in case, take this. If the demon should lash out--"

"I will crack this flask on its head," she said.

"You can throw it down and run," Nik said. "The scent of silver should--"

"I will crack this flask on its head and jam the broken pieces of the bottle in its eyes."

"As you wish."

Nik turned to the chest. It had been elegantly carved and inlaid with precious stones, but in the damp cave its wood swelled and split. He lifted the latch and eased the lid open.

The man in the casket was nothing like the demon he'd seen in the dream. He had the look of a vigorous older man gone to seed, with thick, well-muscled limbs, a rounded belly, and iron grey hair. He had a full beard not unlike old statues of the pagan god Zeus. But even in the sleep of death, or undeath, the old Emperor's lips curled in a cruel sneer. Nik trembled, and he hoped the cold eyes would not open, for he did not want to gaze upon the dark spirit of such a man in death.

Cassia looked over his shoulder and hissed. "That's him. What should we do?"

"We need to cut out his heart," Nik said.

"Very well. Dominus, would you like to do the honors?"

Acrisius edged his way towards the chest. Beads of sweat appeared on his brow, and he cursed under his breath. He stopped a few feet away.

"Such a chore seems like it would ill suit a man of rank such as myself," Acrisius said. "And the proper handling of the dead is a job for women and clergy. I'll... wait outside in a respectful vigil."

"Whatever you desire, dominus," Cassia said, bowing her head. Nik doubted Acrisius heard her, as he had dropped his gladius and fled.

Nik sighed and picked up the short sword. "Well, it should be easier the second time."

He hacked through the ribcage, slicing the thick, ropey tendons that held the heart in place. He kept himself from vomiting at the smell of the corpse's innards, but only just. He reached into the stinking gore and pulled out a slimy black organ from the strigoi's chest. He held it at arms' length.

"Give it to me," Cassia said.

He did as she asked, puzzled.

"It's worth a try," she said. "It worked for you." She lifted the lid from a salt barrel.

The desiccated corpse inside was pitifully small. A boy, Nik thought, though he could not be sure. The child's flesh was dried and crusted with salt, and his mouth open as though he was still screaming. A rope bound his feet. His throat was slashed, the same cut farmers used to bleed pigs before they were butchered.

Cassia knelt beside the corpse. She did not shy away from its horrors but lifted the poor child's head as tenderly as a mother. She cut off a piece of the strigoi's heart, placed it inside the child's mouth and closed it again. She did the same for each of the other two corpses, which were as small and sad as the first. One had a carved wooden toy still clutched in its hands.

Nik didn't know what to expect. She had fed him a sliver of the strigoi's heart, and he had recovered his injuries. But the children had been dead for so long--days, weeks, perhaps even months. But the church said the Son of Man had raised the dead, and he had seen incredible magics. So, he watched and waited.

Nothing happened.

"Let's go," Nik said. "There's nothing more we can do. We'll bury them in the morning."

"No," Cassia whispered. "We can't leave them alone in the dark." Tears streaked her face.

He wanted to put an arm around her to comfort her, but he sensed that was the wrong thing to do, that his touch would remind her of other, darker things than he intended. Instead, he asked her for the flask of sanctified water, which she gave him without a word. He anointed the small bodies with the holy water and a few sprinkles of myrrh. He made the sign of the cross and said a prayer for each one. As he spoke Cassia calmed.

"It's time," Nik said, and he took her hand to lead her out of the cave. But before they could go, he heard a noise, a sound like coughing. They turned. A black-haired boy, a living child, scrambled out of one of the barrels.

"Stop!" the boy said. "You with the fancy hat! You know how to get out of this fetid hole, right? Don't leave me here, *pathice*!"

Behind him, there was a wail. "I want to go home!" a young girl cried. "Mamma will be mad I'm late and she'll hit me with the spoon!"

"Where am I? Why is it so dark in here? Who are you?" asked a second girl, kicking herself free of the barrel. She marched over to the wailing girl and took her hand with the firm authority of an older sibling.

Nik gave silent thanks to God. His beard was wet with tears. Together, he and Cassia lead the children to the light.

Lantgen

THE KING OF RATS

Nikolas covered his mouth and nose with the hem of his cloak as he entered the town. Behind him, Petros gagged into the sleeve of his cassock. Corpses lay rotting in the streets, some rolled up against buildings to clear the road, others trampled into gory stains by horses' hooves. The freshest bodies were blue-black with plague, their faces contorted into horrors. Swarms of flies hummed in his ears. He swatted them away from his eyes. His mule shied and twitched its withers, flicking its tail to drive off the insects.

He wanted nothing more than to find an inn or tavern or anyplace at all where he could escape the grisly scene and hellish stench and drink himself into a stupor. But the church had sent him here for a reason, so instead he reined in his mule.

"Something's wrong," he said.

"Brilliant observation, master," his apprentice replied between heaving gags. "I do believe many good folk of this wretched burg are quite dead."

Nik rolled his eyes at the sarcasm but refrained from reprimanding the youth. Petros had a keen mind when he could be bothered to use it, but the boy got touchy around plague victims.

"That's not what I meant. There's something missing," he said. He tried to sound calm and impassive, but that was hard to accomplish when while suppressing his urge to vomit.

"Rats," Petros said. "There should be hundreds of them with all the bodies they've left lying around. They should be having a bloody feast." His voice cracked on the last words.

"Indeed," Nikolas said. He hated rats as much as the next man, but the nasty beasts' absence disturbed him. He flicked the reins. Petros tore his gaze away from a woman's bloated corpse and followed him.

The mayor's house, or rather what was left of it, was easy to find. A smoking ruin just off the town square, he only recognized it by the obscene curses someone had chalked on the charred wood. "Our lord mayor," the unnamed artist had written, above a crude picture of a man being burned alive.

"We won't be enjoying his hospitality, then," Petros said, kicking at the rain-sodden ashes. "Wonder what he did to make them that mad."

Nikolas shrugged. "If the prince hasn't appointed a new mayor, that explains the corpses in the street. No one's left to pay corpse-men to collect them or dig graves."

"What about the parish priest?" Petros asked. "Why hasn't he demanded they be buried?"

"He's probably fled town to escape the plague."

Petros glowered. "Maybe that's what we should do, too. It doesn't look like there's anyone left here anyway."

Nik was tempted to agree with Petros. But as he turned away from the burnt house, he caught a glimpse of a face in a nearby window. A girl, perhaps around ten years, thin and pale. He duffed his battered red mitre and bowed. Her eyes opened wide and she pulled away from the window.

"I guess you'll be talking to her before we go," Petros said, staring at the girl.

"It's our duty," Nik replied.

The girl lived in a row house near enough to the fire Nik wondered how it had escaped the blaze. The bottom floor was a carpenter's workshop and market stall. Half-finished furniture and broken barrels were strewn about, looking grey and woebegone. Nik and Petros climbed up the stairs to the living quarters and knocked on the door.

"Kom nicht rein! Keine Krankheit hier!" A woman's voice called through the door.

"Great, she only speaks the goat-grunting common tongue they use here. How are we supposed to talk to them?" Petros asked.

"I'll try a little Frankish with her," Nik answered. He had a good ear for languages, but he'd never visited the Northern kingdoms before. No one answered his Frankish, nor his Greek, though that did not surprise him. He tried some Slavic tongues, but to little avail. In desperation, he tried speaking Latin, and to his surprise, he got a quiet answer in a piping voice.

A round-faced blonde woman opened the door, her face unreadable. She held on tightly to the girl from the window, who leaned against a rough wooden crutch. A man stood beside them, his shoulders slumped and his head bent over like a wilted flower.

"You can understand me, little lady?" Nik asked.

"Yes, sir. I studied Latin at the convent before it was closed," the girl replied. She stared at his red bishop's hat in disbelief. "Why are you here?"

"This is where God called me," he said. It was a better answer than a long-winded spiel about church politics and fragile negotiations between the Greek and Latin worlds, and perhaps it was true enough, in its way. "I'm here to help."

The girl shook her head. "There's no one left to help. They're all gone."

"Who is all gone?" he asked.

"All the other children. The rats, too, of course."

"Where did they go?" Nik asked.

The girl hesitated, and the slump-shouldered man raised his head. He had a burn that stretched down the side of his face and neck.

"Hell," the man said in a weak rasp. "He took them to Hell."

"We heard the plague was coming long before it reached us," the burnt man said in a broken pidgin of Frankish and Latin. He'd convinced the woman to open a keg of ale for them, though it took a great deal of arguing. She had taken her daughter and retreated upstairs the second the ale was open and refused to come down again. "As mayor, I took precautions. We didn't allow travellers from plague-infected areas to enter the town. I hired a local astrologer to predict when the plague would end, and..." He looked sideways at Nikolas' mitre.

"Please, continue. I will consider anything you tell me to be in the spirit of confession," Nik said. He took a sip of ale. It had soured, so the woman had stirred bitter herbs into it to mask the taste.

"I asked one of the wise women for help. She said rats spread the plague. I could keep travellers out until my dying breath, but that wouldn't stop the plague unless I got rid of the rats." The mayor downed his cup and poured another. Nik wondered how he could manage to drink the horrid brew without flinching. He took another small sip to be polite.

"Wise words," Nikolas said. "So you hired rat catchers?"

"Not exactly," the mayor said. "Every town from here to Constantinople wanted rat catchers, and they were hard to come by. And expensive."

"What did you do?"

"I offered a bounty. One guilder for every ten rats a freeman could bring me. I thought I'd interest a couple of local fellows, they'd clear out the big nests, I'd give them at most maybe fifty guilders apiece."

"Not a bad plan," Nik said. "Hardly the type of thing that causes townsfolk to burn down a man's house. What went wrong?"

The mayor took huge swig of ale and wiped his mouth on his sleeve. "I didn't expect--there was--I didn't catch the man's name. He called himself the Piper, and he looked...unnatural." The burnt man shifted uncomfortably while Nik raised his eyebrows.

"His robe shifted colors, I mean, even while I watched, that kind of thing. Carried what he called a pipe but mark my words it was a wizard's staff or wand or some such. Had a couple of rough fellows with him too, mercenary types. Asked me about the bounty."

Petros grimaced and clapped his palm to his forehead.

Nik motioned at him to stay quiet. "And you made him the same offer as you'd made everyone else," he said. He made the sign of benediction to encourage the man.

The mayor nodded, staring into his cup as though he wished he could drown himself in it. "I didn't know. He played some song on his pipe I'd never heard, and the rats just came to him.

His fellows scooped them up and counted each one before throwing them in the river to drown. They were at it all day. There wasn't a rat left in the town or even the fields around us for miles. By sunset, he came to me with the final count--ten thousand dead rats. I owed him a thousand guilders."

Nik whistled. Even in the great courts of Constantinople, that would be a significant sum. Surely no one in a town this small had ever seen so much money. The wizard would have been foolish to expect the mayor to have it, and Nik had a terrible feeling that this so-called Piper wasn't foolish at all.

"I begged him to give us time to pay. I gave him the hundred guilders I'd set aside for the job and all the valuables I could scrounge from elsewhere. I even went around town to collect for him, but we're plain folk here. Most people laughed in my face when I asked 'em for gold. Hardly anyone had two coins to rub together."

Nikolas stroked his beard and sighed. He'd doubtless have whiter hair after this.

"Did he ask for the children then?" He said gently. He'd encountered slavers before. They lurked around towns and villages stricken by drought or blight, and waited until people were so hungry, they'd sell their children for a sackful of grain. But this was the first time he'd heard of one using rat-bounties and magic.

The mayor shook his head, or at least it wobbled drunkenly at the top of his neck. He gripped the table as though afraid it would disappear from under him.

"Didn't ask for anything," he said, his voice a hoarse whisper. "Took out his pipe again and--my son, my sweet little boy..." He crossed himself, mumbling in garbled Latin. "Took them all." He swallowed a last swig of ale, then lay his head on the table and closed his eyes.

"Can you find them?" Petros asked. He poked at the mayor to try to wake him, but the man had fallen into a deep stupor. "The piper, I mean. And the children."

"I can try," Nik said. "But I need to talk to the girl. If she heard the song, she might know what he intended to do with the children."

"Good luck convincing her mother to let her talk to you," Petros said.

Nik heard the woman muttering in the room above them, then the scrape of something heavy pushed across the room and set against the door. To keep them out, he suspected. He sighed. It was a wise precaution perhaps--even men of the church might harm a woman alone with a lame child. But it would make talking to the girl difficult.

Night had fallen, clear and cold. Nik looked out the window, but he did not see smoke or the tell-tale spark of a friendly kitchen fire anywhere. Without no inn or hostel, he and Petros made themselves comfortable in the carpenter's workshop. As he drifted off to sleep, he could hear the soft sound of a whispered conversation. A child's voice, lilting and gentle even in the harsh tones of her native tongue. But before he could try to parse her words into something he could translate, he fell asleep.

Petros woke him the next morning. The mayor had disappeared. The boy had scrounged up a few eggs from somewhere. Like many children who'd survived a famine, he'd developed a knack for ferreting out any food that might be hidden nearby. Nik considered this one of the boy's most useful talents, though it often meant giving a few coins to irate farmers with pilfered stores.

"Are there more of these?" he asked.

"A few," Petros answered, giving him a sideways glance.

"Bring them here. We should share our bounty with our neighbors like good Christians."

Petros opened his mouth to protest, then closed it again and nodded. Nik rummaged through the huge rucksack he brought on all his journeys, pulling out a stout staff of olive wood he'd found on his first trip to the Holy Land. He poked at the hearth with his staff and whispered a hidden word, coaxing a fire from the coals he found there.

Petros returned with a trove of eggs and a small sack of dried winter apples. Nik found a heavy cooking pot hanging over the hearth and set to cooking the eggs. A few more whispered words, and the scent of the eggs wafted up through the ceiling to where the mother and daughter lay sleeping. It wasn't long before he heard hushed tones, and the scrape of furniture moving above his head. The door opened.

"Father Bishop?" the girl's voice called.

"Yes, my daughter?" he answered.

"May we...if it pleases you...may we break our fast with you?"

"Of course, my daughter. 'For when I hungered, you fed me.' Come eat your fill."

The girl's mother carried her down the stairs, with deliberate care, cradling the lame child in her arms. Nikolas felt his heart ache as he watched them. He wondered how the missing children fared, and his feeling darkened, as though a shadow passed over his soul.

They shared a small meal together. He waited until the girl sighed in contentment to ask his questions.

"I must know, little daughter--did you hear the song the Piper sang? Could you tell me about it?"

The child frowned. "I heard it." She shook her head from side to side, as though trying to dislodge it from her memory.

"Have you dreamed about it since?"

"Yes, father." She seemed reluctant to say more, and her mother pulled her closer.

"Peace," he said to the mother, smiling and opening his palms. "I can help. I can take the spell out of her and keep the dreams away."

The girl translated for her mother, who nodded.

He pulled a jar out of his sack. "Holy Water," he said to the girl, which was a harmless enough lie. He dripped some on her forehead, as though for a baptism, then coated his hands in the clear liquid and press them against her head as if to give her a blessing.

The suffocating stench of rot and filth filled his nostrils. He struggled to breathe. So dark. The stone, rough and cold. There were moans and skittering sounds. The sharp crack of a whip. Sobbing. A Cave. Where? He couldn't tell, but they hadn't moved far. They were waiting, waiting for slave merchants or the whip or the hungry skittering things to take them...

Nik gasped. He jerked away from the girl and clutched his throat. He heard Petros cursing, felt the boy's thin hands push against his chest. Thick black muck welled up inside him, drowning him. He rolled onto his side, choking and coughing. Petros wiped his face with the edge of his cassock and tipped some of the "holy water" into his mouth. He coughed and spluttered, heaving in great gulps of air.

"Master? Master?" Petros cried, shaking him. "Father Nikolas? Are you...?" The boy's face worked.

"Shhh, shhh, my boy," Nik said. "I'll survive. It's vile magic that Piper brews, but I'll recover."

Petros wiped his tears away with an angry fist. "You shouldn't have...stupid do-gooder priest!"

It wasn't Petros' usual string of curses, so Nik decided to let it go. The rats, he thought. He'd been drowning like the rats. If the piper had drowned them at all, and it wasn't some trickery.

"The river," Nik said. "We've got to get to the river." He bowed to the girl and her mother to take his leave. After he left, they would find the bag of coins he'd hidden inside a shoe the girl had left near the hearth. He hoped it would be enough to keep them safe and fed.

At the river, Nik swirled the water with his staff, hoping to find the threads of the Piper's spell hidden in the wild, rain-swollen waters. Nothing. He stroked his beard, then took out a packet of herbs, a gift from an elderly nun who'd been a wood-witch before she entered a convent. Old Sibel had watery eyes that had gone white-blind, but she spoke and moved with the assurance of a wise woman, and she had a gift for clear-seeing that bordered on prophecy.

He pulled a few leaves from Sibel's bundle and crumpled them into a wooden pipe he kept in his cassock. He lit the pipe with his staff, then inhaled the sweet vapors.

Nik's eyes softened and his sight blurred until it looked as though the world was covered in a thick mist, but his other senses grew keener. He could smell the rot from the dead and the smoke from the fire that burned the mayor's house. But he could also make out, dimly, scents from living people. He inhaled slowly, searching for the scent of magic, crisp and bright like fresh green apples ripening in the sun.

He gagged. There was a taste of magic in the air, but it was nothing clean or natural. It smelled wrong, as though the magic had rotted in the veins of the wizard-piper, like a fruit that fermented after being left on the ground too long.

"Stay vigilant," he told Petros.

"I take it that means you're about to do something stupid," Petros said.

Nikolas reminded himself that patience and serenity were among the loveliest Christian virtues. He knelt by the riverbank, sniffing and listening.

"Doesn't it seem strange to you that there aren't any dead rats floating around here?" he asked. He hadn't seen any before taking Sibel's herb, and he couldn't smell any now.

"They could have floated away..."

"All of them? Not one got caught in the rushes or washed up along the shore?"

Petros frowned. "That is strange, but not impossible," the boy said. His dark eyes glinted with fierce intelligence. "And there's something else. Why would he kill the rats anyway? He didn't need to if he was going to take the children no matter. He surely knew the mayor would never be able to pay."

"My thoughts exactly," Nik said.

"So, he wanted the rats for something else. Blood sacrifice?"

"I don't think so. I think they were a test. Send the rats through a magic gate, make sure most of them were alive on the other side. That kind of magic is tricky--he'd have to align the gates perfectly in order to keep the rats from coming out in pieces or ending up stuck in a rock, especially if he was sending them to a cave. He'd have plenty of time to check on the rats while the poor mayor ran about town trying to collect his money. Once he'd fine-tuned the gate..."

171

"He could bring the children though. Their parents would have no way to find them," Petros scowled and kicked hard at a riverstone along the bank. "Filthy devil-spawned slave-trading demon pigs."

Nik didn't see any reason to correct the boy's language in this case. "He's covered his tracks well. There's only one way into the cave."

"Oh no," Petros groaned. "Master, don't tell me..."

"Now Petros," Nik said. "Don't worry. I won't bring you-- it's too dangerous. I just need you to wait here in case the children need some help coming back through."

Petros narrowed his eyes and gave his master a keen, hawk-like glance. At last the boy nodded. "As you wish," he said.

Nik stuffed a few flasks of potion and a bit more of Sibel's herb into his cassock and took a firm grip on the olive wood staff. He tried not to flinch as he stepped into the icy water. The current was strong, and it tugged on his shivering flesh as he waded deeper into the river. He leaned into his staff. His feet went numb and he struggled to avoid tripping over sharp rocks. The water came up to his chest, then his shoulders. Nik hesitated and felt ahead with his staff.

"Perhaps I've made a---" His staff caught in a swirl of water. He felt a powerful undertow, then his feet slipped, and he was gone.

He found himself in a dark so deep he wondered if he'd fallen all the way to hell, drenched and shivering. But no, there were voices echoing off the walls around him, ordinary human voices. Children's voices, some crying, some whispering like dried husks of straw in a winter wind.

Nik considered lighting a fire or otherwise trying to make some light but decided firmly against it--he'd alert the wizard.

He fumbled in his cassock for Sibel's herb, chewing a few of the wet leaves. Sibel'd warned him that could make the effects more potent, but that was just as well. It tasted like a strange combination of coriander seeds and licorice root.

As his ears sharpened, he began to hear other noises in the cave as well. Scratching. Rustling. And every once in a while, a squeak that echoed off the stone walls of the cave. Rats. Why would the piper keep them alive after they'd served their purpose?

The children were easy to smell--even unwashed and filthy the sweet tang of childhood clung to them. The others, no so much--they stank of soured ale and pox sores. Even worse was the Piper's magic, which had a sulfurous stench that turned his stomach.

Nik considered the situation. As far as he could tell, there were only two guards down the tunnel where the children were kept, but should one of those men yell for help, everyone in the cave would hear. Then again, even with a guttering candle, they couldn't see very well in the dark. And they weren't expecting him.

He took out one of his potions and added a pinch of valerian and a sprinkle of lemon balm. He swirled the liquid until it smelled like flowers and honey, then tapped it with his staff and murmured a few words. He arranged his expression into the serene, gentle smile that he used to calm nervous horses, and stuffed his bishop's mitre in his cassock. As he approached the men, he thudded his heels to the floor. The easy, confident sound of his stride made them relax, even as they looked for him in the darkness of the cave. He stopped just far enough away to keep his face in shadows.

One of the guards drew a rusted sword. "Password?"

Nik shook his head. Sibel's potion made the two guards seem bleary and unfocused, but that might trick the guards into believing him drunk.

He slurred his words. "I'm not here for my shift. The boys just thought you'd like a drop of the sweet stuff his highness brought for us." He pulled the flask of potion out of his robe. His spell gave it the golden look of fine metheglin.

"Mighty generous of 'em," said the second guard. He sat up slowly, but with the kind of deadly grace Nik associated with foxes. "I ne'er heard of any of those louts parting with the good stuff without a fight."

Nik laughed, trying to sound easy. "They wouldn't have, except they've near blacked out already. Didn't want you fellows beating the tar out of them when you found out you'd been left out."

The first guard shrugged. "Fair enough then." He tore the potion out of Nik's hand and took a deep swig. "That is the good stuff! I've not tasted such sweetness in..." He toppled forward, the rusted sword dropping from limp hands.

Too much valerian, Nikolas thought. He raised his staff just in time to block the second guard's swing, then thrust it at the blurry place he thought might be the guard's throat. The man dodged. Nik whirled the staff, hoping to catch the guard unprepared, but the man ducked under his swing and lunged. Nik stepped back, dipping and turning to avoid the guard's sword. The man sneered, pushing forward at Nik like an amorphous shadow. Desperate, Nik swung the staff low and felt it clobber against the guard's knee.

The man let out a pained yell as he went down. He rolled on the ground, clutching his knee. Nik shoved his staff between the man's teeth to keep him from yelling, then poured the potion down his throat.

Nik wiped sweat from his brow and leaned against the cave wall. He felt old, too old, but there were children who needed him, so he pulled himself together and hurried deeper into the cave. He'd knocked over the guards' candle, plunging himself into absolute darkness once again. All around him he heard the rustling, scurrying sound of the rats. He reached his hand out to feel the cave wall and felt his fingers brush against a mangy, wormlike tail.

He nearly stumbled over the first child he found. Boy or girl, he couldn't tell. A few murmured words and the child's ropes fell away. Nik helped the child to his or her feet, and felt a small hand take hold of his. He breathed a sigh of relief. He'd always had a gift for calming children, and they seemed to trust him, but he couldn't be sure they wouldn't panic or scream in such a terrifying place as this. He unbound them, one after another, whispering for them to hold hands and stay close.

He'd freed nearly twenty when he felt prickles forming on the back of his neck. The magic--it smelled different now. Hot and metallic, like a blacksmith's forge. He listened. Where were the rats? They'd followed him to the children, but now they'd disappeared.

"Quickly," he whispered to the children. "Help me free the others!" He could not bear to leave anyone behind, but he did not dare take much time. When all the children had been freed, he risked a light. Sibel's potion had worn off so he could use his eyes, and it would help guide the young ones. He tapped his staff against the ground and hummed a tune deep in his chest. The top of his staff lit up like a beacon.

The children blinked and rubbed their eyes, and for the first time Nik saw their faces, filthy and terrified, some bleeding, broken, or bruised. White hot rage bloomed inside him, but now was not the time for that.

He gave them a serene smile he did not feel and beckoned them to follow him. If he could reach the gate, he could get them through. They rushed past the sleeping guards, but now he could hear shouts, heavy footsteps, and the ring of chainmail.

"This way!" he whispered, pointing to the gate. In the dim light of his staff, it gave off a watery shimmer. But it was too late--the men were coming. "Whatever happens, keep going!" he said, still smiling serenely at the children. So many! Too many to get them all through the gate before the armed men fell upon them.

Nik pulled out his last flask of potion. He warmed it in the light of the staff and sprinkled in a pinch of crushed black peppers. The potion turned a vivid red and bubbled furiously.

He waited until he could see the glint of armor and raised swords, then poured the potion in a line along the ground. It bloomed into a wall of dancing flame. The men drew back, flinching as the fire heated their armor, some dropping weapons and cursing.

Nik glanced back at the children. Most made it out, but two straggled behind. A large-boned boy dragged his broken leg along the floor of the cave while a small girl struggled to help him, pulling at him and cursing. Nik rushed over. He picked up the boy and groaned. The child had the strapping build of a well-fed young ox. With the girl's help, Nik managed to get the injured boy to the gate as his spell flickered out. He pushed the boy through. The girl followed, her hands wrapped firmly around the boy's arm. But before Nik could follow them, something heavy thunked against his skull, and he knew no more.

It was the smell that woke him--a horrid mix of putrid meat with the acrid tang of urine. He kept his eyes closed, listening. Scrabbling sounds, and horrid little screeches. Nearby, heavy breathing.

"I know you're not asleep," a man's voice said. Unlike the rest of the foul cave, the voice was clear and pure as fresh water, its lilting, melodic tones so beautiful his heart ached with longing. He wanted to trust that voice, follow it, do as it asked.

He forced himself to open his eyes. The Piper had a delicate, pointed chin and hair that fell to his shoulders in soft, dark waves. He looked young, but felt ancient, like a spray of new leaves on a primordial tree. His robes flowed around him as though stirred by a gentle breeze, scintillating as a silver trout. His hands moved with fluid grace over a wooden flute.

Nik twitched his nose. For all his beauty, for all the ways Nik wanted nothing more than to please this man, to follow him, he felt wrong somehow. Pins and needles ran up his arms from the tight ropes that bound his hands behind his back. And the smell. There was something wrong with the smell.

A skittering sound drew his gaze. Black rats, squirming in rot and piss and muck. They swarmed in a great ball, their worm tails matted together with muck and hair. Bile rose in his throat.

The Piper tapped lightly on his flute, and the rats swarmed around him. "You took them from me," he said.

Nik shivered. "Please," he choked out. He wanted to obey that voice, to beg it for forgiveness, to tell it everything, but when he closed his eyes, he saw the children escaping, bedraggled and desperate. He thought of Petros, pulling them to shore, waiting by the river for Nik to emerge. His heart quailed within his chest, but he could not betray them.

"I see you need more convincing," the Piper said. "I searched for them, of course. They couldn't have gotten far without help. There must have been someone else on the other side of the gate. Someone who helped them get away, who helped hide them. Tell me. Who was with you? Where did they go?" He put the flute to his lips.

The music was soft and haunting. It flowed from the pipe like fog from the sea, enveloping Nik's mind. Memories played in his head. The rocky shores of the town where he'd been born. Swirling hot sands of the Holy Land. The grand basilica of Constantinople. Petros, climbing out of a wooden barrel, the first time they'd met. Petros following him into the town, gagging into his sleeve...

"NO!" Nik screamed. He writhed in his bounds, accidentally banging his head. For a brief moment, the pain drove the infernal music out of his head.

"Stop that," the Piper sang. He touched the flute to his lips once more, and Nik felt the fog slipping over him, lulling him...

He smashed his face against the rocky cave floor. Pain bloomed in his nose as clear and bright as the star above Bethlehem.

The Piper put down his flute, and traced a long, elegant finger along Nik's cheek. "Your nose is broken," he said, his voice no longer melodic but cold and ancient, like something that had crawled out of a deep hole in the earth. "I can break other parts of you, too. Or feed them to my little friends."

The rat king chittered and drew closer to Nik. The stench made his eyes water. Scaly paws crawled up his arms and chest. Beady black eyes stared into his, bearing rows of sharp little teeth.

"Kyrie eleison," Nik whispered. "Christe eleison." He wondered if he had the strength to be a martyr.

"Start with his eyes," the Piper said, soft and dangerous.

Nik writhed and bucked, trying to shake the horrid beasts off, but they clung to his chest. One of the largest rats, a mangy, scabbed little monster the size of a small cat, dug its claws into his beard. The last thing he would see would be its grimy teeth chewing through his eyelids. As if to taunt him, the rat paused to lick the blood spurting from his broken nose, drinking it up with lascivious abandon. He screamed.

But he wasn't the only one screaming. The Piper filled the cave with deafening shrieks. The rats on Nik paused, looking back at their master. He was fighting a weedy, adolescent figure armed with nothing more than an iron chain and a flickering torch.

"Call your rats off my master, or I'll...I'll...give you a birching you'll never forget!" Petros yelled. He swung the chain in a wide arch over his head, then slammed it into the Piper's face. The iron left red scorch marks where it touched his skin.

The Piper howled in rage. Leaving Nik, the rats swarmed Petros. The boy beat at them with his chain, but they slipped by him. They climbed his legs and clung to his cassock.

Nik struggled against his bonds but couldn't free himself. Already the Piper was dusting himself off, and the look in his eyes made Nik's bowls shrivel. His mind worked furiously.

"The torch, Petros!" he shouted. "Set them on fire!"

Petros stopped whirling his chains and waved his torch at the conjoined tails of the rat king. The matted fur and dried dung that linked the rats blazed up. Rats screamed and pulled against their entwined tails, sending the rat king spinning. Freed rats scurried away.

The Piper gnashed his teeth, diving at Petros. But Nik rolled across the floor, throwing himself at the evil wizard's feet. The Piper tripped. Petros darted forward, wrapping him in the iron chain. It gave an ominous rattle. The Piper fought like a wild animal. His exposed skin hissed and popped, and his shrieks grew wild. A bright light flashed, then he was gone.

"Where did he go?" Petros asked. He unbound Nik, and together they searched through a stinking heap of ashes.

"I do not know," Nik said. "But that is a mystery for another day." He knelt and took Petros' hands in his. "I give thanks to God for the day I found you, my dear boy. If you hadn't--"

"Stop," Petros said. Even in the dim light of the cave, Nik could see the boy's blush. "I did one small thing to repay the debt I owe you."

Nik thought about arguing but decided against it. Instead he whispered a few thankful prayers for the boy's safety and courage. Then he rose to his feet.

"Let's get out of here," he said, more weary than he'd felt since his days on the Emperor's infernal councils.

"Really? You'd like to go? I was just beginning to appreciate the bouquet de rat," Petros answered.

Nikolas had to stop himself from laughing. It made his broken nose hurt too much.

VERY SHORT STORIES

Very short stories are a fun way to play with ideas and be creative on social media. They are stories written in a tweet, often with hashtags like #vss365 or #satsplat. You can find more on the Lunarian Press website and my twitter account, @TheWise Serpent.

Difficult Magic

No wonder magic was so difficult, she thought. The spells were all horribly vague, completely unlike the clear scientific language she was used to. Twelve cattails? She squinted. The tails of actual cats, or the water plants? No way to tell. She sighed.

The Cure

The cauldron boiled and seethed. Frothy black effervescence floated to the top. She sprinkled a couple of milky eyes into the brew. At last, when the smell burnt her nostrils, she poured him a tumbler full.

"There," she said. "The strongest hangover cure I can make."

Butterflies

The delicate butterflies flit over the surface of the lake, their wings silver and blue in the moonlight. They float around the waterfall and vanish in the mist.

"Where do they go?" I whisper.

"No one knows," Gran says. "But mayhap the fairies."

Waif

They always send a waif, he thought. Skinny, dirty, a supposed virgin with no family or connections. He flicked his tongue at the latest sacrifice. Her eyes burned bright.

"I can unlock the gates," she said. "You could feast on the others, the rich, fat ones."

Willow

"WILLOW! Bring me that antidote!" His slave stumbled into the room, tripping over her feet. He poked her with his cane.

"Hurry!" Her hands shook as she poured a drink into his mouth. He cursed.

"Wrong one, stupid girl!" He fell, his mouth foaming.

Willow smiled.

Acknowledgements

Thank you to everyone who inspired, encouraged, and helped me to write this book.

Thank you in particular to my beta readers, Sarah Mensinga, Gerardo Delgadillo, my mother Kristine Lantgen, and my sister Vanessa Hicks. Your feedback and encouragement were so helpful in the creation of this book.

Thank you as well to the magazines and editors of Phantaxis, the Gallery of Curiosities, and Swords and Sorcery Magazine, who first published Elven Carols, There Was a Nicholas Once, and Braids. When I was discouraged, having those stories appear in print kept me going.

Special thanks to my husband David Farmer for creating such a beautiful book cover. Your support has been invaluable, and I'm so amazed by your talent and creativity. I'm thankful every day for our beautiful family.

Author Bio

Alexis Lantgen is a writer, teacher, and classical musician. She loves Renaissance Faires and all things science fiction and fantasy. Her first book, *Sapience: A Collection of Science Fiction Short Stories*, is available on Amazon from Lunarian Press. Her work has appeared in the Gallery of Curiosities, Phantaxis, Red Sun Magazine, and Swords and Sorcery Magazine. Her nonfiction articles have appeared in Renaissance Magazine. Alexis is occasionally on twitter @TheWiseSerpent and has been spotted once in a blue moon on Instagram. She lives with her husband, her two beautiful, spirited children, and two very patient cats in Texas.

More from Lunarian Press

For updates on more fantastic fiction, author events, calls for submissions, and more:

VISIT OUR WEBSITE

www.lunarianpress.com

FOLLOW US ON TWITTER

@LunarianPress

EMAIL US

lunarianpressbooks@gmail.com

www.ingramcontent.com/pod-product-compliance
Lightning Source LLC
Chambersburg PA
CBHW032006170626
46807CB00006B/2681